The Calling

A Paranormal Mystery

I0531383

Daria Kacie

~Join our mailing for updates and special offers.~

Quantumlifepublishing.com

Facebook.com/DariaKacie

DEDICATION

To my family and friends who have supported me in all my endeavors, big and small.

TABLE OF CONTENTS

Dedication..3

Chapter 1 5

Chapter 2 8

Chapter 3 18

Chapter 4 25

Chapter 5 33

Chapter 6 38

Chapter 7 48

Chapter 8 52

Chapter 9 62

Chapter 10 68

Chapter 11 71

Chapter 12 74

Chapter 13 79

Chapter 14 84

Chapter 15 95

Chapter 16 117

Chapter 17 119

Chapter 18 130

Chapter 19 138

Chapter 20 145

About The Author.................................146

One Last thing 146

Join Our Reader List.............................146

CHAPTER 1

Karen, happy to have a day off after working a long night shift at the hospital, caught up on some housework. Her brown wavy hair loosely pulled back, she avoided make up for the day. Karen walked briskly to the door having heard four knocks. Swinging the door open, ready to greet the visitor, she found only empty space.

Kids, she thought. Stepping outside into the warm sun, the street was empty and silent. She needed to get the laundry folded before Brandi and Billy, her children, arrived home from school. Karen loved her little house. She bought it two years prior after her divorce. It had not been easy to end her 15 year marriage but she knew she had to for her sanity. Being single had it's challenges but she was proud of her accomplishments and had a positive view about her future. A diehard romantic, Karen knew the right man was out there for her. She folded the cloths separating them into three baskets.

Bam! Bam! Bam! Bam! The aggressive pounding on her front door pierced the silence once again. Looking out the windows this time as she rushed to the door, she saw no one outside. She whipped open the door and was once again met with empty space. "Knock it off you kids or I'll be talking to your parents!" she yelled into the empty street. Back in the laundry room, she began folding the final basket of clothes. Slamming the shirt on the counter she folded it very precisely and pressed it into Billy's basket. Bam! Bam! Bam! Bam! This time, the knocking came aggressively, form behind her. The sound did not come from

5

outside, it came from inside. Her muscles tensed from the shock of the sound to the point of pain. She had no time to think. She bolted through the house and right out the front door into the middle of her lawn. Standing in the middle of the yard, trying to catch her breath, she wondered what had just happened. Billy and Brandi stopped on the sidewalk when they saw their mother burst through the front door, run to the middle of the yard, and stop.

"Mom? What are you doing?" Brandi asked. Karen wasn't sure what she was doing. She didn't want to alarm the children and she was annoyed at the same time.

"That wasn't funny!" she snapped at Brandi.

"What wasn't funny, Mom?"

"Were you kids around the side of the house just now?"

"No," they both said simultaneously. "Why?"

"It's nothing," Karen said as she headed back into the house. "Get inside and get changed, we have to be at your dad's by 5:00."

Billy, a wiry twelve year old, described as a 'mellow kid' by the adults who loved him looked quickly at his sister. Brandi, a quiet redhead in her senior year of high school made it her business to watch out for her little brother. They both rolled their eyes at each other as they went to their rooms to change clothes and get ready to leave for the weekend. Karen pushed herself to the back of the couch attempting to slow down her pounding heart by breathing through her nose. *Maybe it was a pipe*, she thought. *Houses settle, right? Yes, they settle and make noise, that's all it is. On the other hand, maybe it was one of the neighbor kids messing around.* Feeling some relief and concluding that she was overreacting to noises made by a settling house, she grabbed her purse and put on some lipstick.

Karen's thoughts raced through her mind as she drove the children to their father's house. Her eyes darted around, landing on passing cars and their drivers but all she could think about was the knocking. She was wondered why she had felt so scared and ended up in the middle of the yard. *Fight or flight*, she thought, *apparently, I'm a "flighter".*

"Mom? Mom!" Brandi raised her voice to get Karen's attention.

"What?" Karen snapped back.

"God! What's wrong Mom?"

"Nothing Brandi, I just have a lot on my mind and want to make sure I have you to your dad's on time." Brandi, seeing her mother's obvious agitation decided she didn't need to poke Mama Bear. She wanted to ask more questions about why they found her in the middle of the yard when they got home from school but decided not to pursue it any further.

Karen waved as her children entered their father's house. She drove home having been gone less than an hour. Approaching the front door, a strange feeling of uneasiness crept into her belly. She opened the door slowly and could hear water running.

What is going on? She said to herself as she approached the kitchen. The water was running full blast into the kitchen sink. *There is no way I left this on, or did I?*

She turned the water off in the kitchen and then could hear the water running in the bathroom. Feeling her stomach begin to tie into a tight knot, Karen cautiously walked toward the bathroom. The water in the sink and bathtub were running full blast. She quickly shut the water down and rushed for the door. Like wringing a cloth out, she felt her insides begin to twist and tighten. She tried to ignore it but she couldn't shake the feeling that someone or something was watching her. She grabbed her purse and keys and locked the door. It seemed like her feet barely touched the ground as she quickly slid into her car. She headed to Lizzy's house.

CHAPTER 2

"Hellooooo!" sang Lizzy as she opened the door to find Karen waiting outside. "What's up?"

"I just dropped the kids off at their dad's and didn't feel like spending Friday night alone with nothing to do."

"Well come on in," Lizzy motioned Karen through the door. "I don't know that it will be all that exciting here but we can figure out something to do!"

Karen and Lizzy, friends since high school, knew pretty much everything about each other. Lizzy had been a year ahead in school but only three months older. With the big "Four O" coming they joked they would hover at 39 for a few years before officially 'crossing over'. It was a long-standing relationship with over 25 years of history. Lizzy and Karen were more than friends; they were family. Karen generally felt she could tell Lizzy anything and everything. Over the years, she had done just that. As she sorted out how to tell Lizzy what had happened and why she had come over but was petering out. She was beginning to feel a little silly about her earlier experience at home. *The kids must have left the water on in the bathroom when they were changing,* she thought trying to convince herself there was a logical explanation.

One of things Lizzy always admired about Karen is that she wasn't uptight. She was steady, positive and dependable. When she arrived, Lizzy noticed her face looked strained. Her energy was off and Lizzy knew it.

"What's up? You seem weird," Lizzy's feelings were usually right on.

"Nothing, I'm tired is all," Karen said as convincingly as she could. She decided that she had no desire to get into the story. She wanted to forget it and believe her house was settling, or kids were playing tricks in the neighborhood. It was just like Karen to hold back. Lizzy broke open a bottle of red wine. Karen began to relax after the first glass. *Surely, I let my imagination run away with me,* Karen thought. She decided to leave it alone and enjoy the evening. After the second glass of wine, Lizzy convinced Karen to stay over and Karen was happy to do so. Even though she had decided she had been overreacting earlier, she had no desire to to go home, by herself, and confront her house in the dark.

Lizzy was starting to feel the onset of a good wine buzz. She cranked up some George Thorogood and started belting out Bad to the Bone while playing air guitar in the middle of the living room. Both now laughing they chatted about their week. In typical Karen fashion, she left the day's incident out of the conversation. Karen held things inside just a little too long as far as Lizzy was concerned. When she would finally reveal a difficult situation, it had usually been going on for quite some time. This trait was a little maddening for Lizzy but after 25 years, she was used to it. The evening wore on with the women singing and dancing through the house. They finally turned in about 2:00 a.m.

Turned out to be a pretty good Friday night after all, thought Karen as she drifted off to sleep. The next thing Karen noticed was the smell of coffee hitting her nostrils.

"And I'm up!" she said jumping from the bed with her arms in the air like a gymnast on her final dismount. Lizzy was at the kitchen table holding her head.

"Seriously," Karen said, "you're hung over?"

"I know, I know," Lizzy whispered loudly. "I'm a light weight! It saves me from alcoholism…"

The statement wasn't too far from the truth. Addiction ran rampant through her family tree. The price she paid for even the

9

slightest bit of overindulgence kept her from drinking much or often.

"Well, your 'George' was in a party mood last night!" Karen said chuckling at her friend.

Lizzy smiled and sipped her coffee as she pointed to the cup on the counter.

"Get yourself a cup of coffee but if you're going to insist on talking, do it quietly."

Karen shook her head as she poured her coffee. "Thanks for the slumber party. It was a fun night."

"No problem. You know I live to entertain you!" Lizzy winced and went back to sipping her coffee. There was little talking for the next half hour as Lizzy nursed her hang over.

Lizzy's head was throbbing as she stood at the door and waved goodbye to Karen. She took one look in the mirror and figured she should comb her hair and wash the makeup off her eyes. She made a piece of toast and decided staying up wasn't an option. She had just crawled back into bed hoping to fall back to sleep when the phone rang. It was Karen.

"Lizzy, " she began to cry, "Lizzy, you have to come over here right now!"

"What's wrong?" Lizzy could hear panic in Karen's voice.

"Please just get here right now! I'm in my car in the driveway."

Lizzy downed some aspirin and quickly threw on jeans and a T-shirt. She was in such a rush she didn't realize her shirt was inside out. *What could be wrong this early in the morning?* Her friend was in some kind of trouble, that's all she needed to know.

Lizzy's car slid a little in the gravel driveway as she parked behind Karen's car. Karen immediately jumped out of her car. When Lizzy saw her, she panicked, thinking one of the kids had been hurt or someone had died. Karen's eyes were red from crying and her face was ashen.

"What in the world?" Lizzy gasped as she pulled her friend into a bear hug. Karen began to cry again and was having a hard time catching her breath.

"Breathe! Breathe! It will be ok. Tell me what's happening!"

Karen leaned against her car and took a couple of deep breaths. She pointed toward the house. Lizzy could see the front door was open. "Were you robbed?" Karen shook her head no. "Is someone in there?" Lizzy asked in alarm. Karen shrugged her shoulders.

Karen finally croaked, "I don't know what is going on and I'm not sure I can go in the house." Lizzy raised her left eyebrow, clearly confused.

"When I got home," Karen said softly, "and opened the door..." she trailed off. Karen gathered herself together, grabbed Lizzy's hand and began walking slowly toward the door.

At the entrance Karen stopped. The two women peered inside. Lizzy could see right away there was something wrong. She could see the dining room chairs laying in the living room forming the shape of a cross. In front of the door, all of Karen's pictures that had hung on the living room walls were stacked neatly in a pile. "Do you hear that?" Karen whispered, "The water is running again."

"Again?" Lizzy whispered back. Karen nodded. Lizzy began playing scenarios in her mind. *Had some kids had broken into the house the night before to play a prank?* Lizzy slowly pulled the screen door, squeaking as it opened. Karen reached out and stopped her.

"Lizzy, I don't think I can go in there."

Lizzy's mind began to race. *What if they were still in there?* "You're right. I'm going to call the police."

Karen nodded and they both ran for Karen's car. Lizzy climbed into the passenger seat and quickly locked her door as Karen locked the others and called 911. Fifteen minutes later two large police officers in crisp dark blue uniforms arrived and cautiously entered the house. It was empty. All the water faucets were on full tilt. The officers searched each room, turning the faucets off as they went. They couldn't help but notice the pile of pictures on the living room floor along with dining room chairs that seemed staged to look like a cross. The chairs were in the middle of the living room on their backs with their feet touching.

Walking through the kitchen they found all the cupboards and drawers in the house opened or pulled out onto the floor. Clearly, something had gone on in the house but neither officer knew what exactly. With a little coaxing, they were able to get Karen into the house to confirm whether anything was missing. Karen verified that everything was still there. It didn't appear that one thing was missing and the Officers found that strange. They made their report of a break in, a break in with no forced entry.

"Are you sure you didn't leave the door unlocked when you left last night?" The taller of the two officers asked Karen.

"No! I know I locked up!"

"Some kids probably noticed you weren't home and decide to play a trick on you. There does not appear to be any evidence of forced entry. Usually in cases like this a door or window has been left open. They look for an easy mark essentially, and then have a party at the owner's expense."

"I'm not sure that makes sense to me," said Lizzy. "What kids come into a house, take nothing, leave the booze untouched, take pictures off the walls and turn on all the water? Doesn't sound like any kind of party we ever had!"

Karen began doubting herself. She had left hastily and was shook up from the knocking she heard the day before. *No, I am sure I locked up. Plus, why was the water running again? I know I did not do that.*

"No. I am sure I locked up before I left," Karen said very pointedly.

The Officers were nice enough to turn the water off in the kitchen and bathrooms. They helped move the chairs back to the dining room table. They made it clear they believed the whole thing was neighborhood kids messing around.

As the shorter, and more attractive of the two officers headed out the door, he remarked to Lizzy, "Nice shirt." She saw a big white smile pull across his face and a little mischief in his eyes.

Lizzy looked down, and for the first time realized her shirt was inside out. She felt her face getting hot and rolled her eyes as she remarked back sarcastically, "Same to ya."

"I'm Dan," he said as he pulled a card from his dark blue pocket and handed it to Lizzy. Lizzy knew her face was bright red by now as the embarrassment of her clothing mishap sunk in. *What a dork!* She chastised herself. *Here I am with this attractive officer and I'm standing here like a dolt, hung over, no makeup and my shirt inside out! Oh God! And my hair!* It was almost too much for her to stand. She tried to act cool but was sure she was not pulling it off.

"If you hear of anything or about anyone who might have done this, give me call," Dan said now with a more serious demeanor.

"Sure," said Lizzy avoiding his gaze.

"Uh, regardless, if you'd like, just call me," he said a little nervously.

"Uh, OK but isn't it your job to 'hear' and find out 'who' did this?" Lizzy shot back, not realizing he was flirting with her.

"We'll do our best but as you can see, there isn't a lot here to go on. Try to have a nice day," said Dan feeling like he blundered moved quickly past her getting to his cruiser as quickly as possible.

She wanted to run screaming into a closet as she watched Officer Dan leave the premises.

Karen sat silently on the couch. Lizzy slumped down next to her and started pulling off her T-shirt to turn it right side out.

"Karen, what do you think is going on here?"

Karen didn't respond.

"Karen, talk to me!" urged Lizzy.

"I think it's a spirit," Karen said flatly.

Now Lizzy was silent.

"Well Lizzy? What do you think of that?"

"I don't know what to think. Are you trying to tell me you think your house is haunted?"

"I don't think some person did this to my house," Karen sighed. "You think I'm crazy don't you?"

"Of course I do!" laughed Lizzy as she took the opportunity to lighten the mood. "I'm kidding Karen. You know, I know, you're not crazy! The thing is, you've never said anything about this. Have you been holding out on me?"

"I never had an issue until yesterday," Karen answered.

"Yesterday? What happened yesterday and why didn't you say something last night?"

"It was a long story I didn't want to go into last night. I thought I was imagining things."

"So, you've been living here for a couple of years, and then all of a sudden you're having paranormal activity in your house?"

"Yes," said Karen. She got up from the couch and moved toward the kitchen as Lizzy followed.

"Has something recently changed? Do you feel threatened?" pushed Lizzy. She felt a little frightened and intrigued.

Karen shrugged her shoulders again as she closed cupboards and pushed drawers back into place. Softly she said, "I don't know what to think. Yesterday, I was alone in the house and I heard knocking. I thought someone was at the door. When I got to the door there was no one there. I was back in the laundry room folding clothes and then four loud knocks sounded like they were right behind me. They sounded like they were coming from inside the room. Then after I dropped the kids off and came home, all the faucets were running full blast. I tried to blow it off like the kids left the water on, but my gut told me that wasn't the case. It all scared the shit out of me! That was one of the reasons I came over to your house."

Lizzy had always been sensitive and had never once felt any weird energy at Karen's house. Lizzy's sensitivity to energy and people had heightened as a teenager. She would often get scared because the anxiety would build insider her to a fevered pitch until she wanted to scream. She could feel something was wrong but never knew exactly what. *How is that helpful?* she had asked God a hundred times. Karen knew that Lizzy had some kind psychic and precognitive abilities. She had known her long enough to see outcomes of many of Lizzy's predictions come true. It never bothered her, but she knew there were times that it did bother Lizzy.

"Do you feel anything?" asked Karen.

"I don't. I'm sorry. I'm not sure what to say. I can say for sure that you're not crazy, but beyond that, I got nothing!"

"I would appreciate you staying here tonight Lizzy," said Karen as she began hanging the pictures back on the wall.

"Well, it's not a problem, but you know this is how all scary movies start, right?" Lizzy said with a smirk.

"Oh shut up Lizzy!"

"No, I'm serious; it's how all scary movies start. Two women innocently brush off some ghostly encounter as a case of the house settling or kids playing tricks and then there is Jason all hockey masked up in the closet waiting to squish our heads or something."

"Lizzy, seriously, shut up!" Karen was obviously not amused.

Lizzy's tone changed quickly to serious, "Karen really, what do you think is going on?"

"I don't know Lizzy. You're the damn psychic, you tell me!"

"You know that isn't my thing. I mean I do feel things sometimes but I don't usually get information like that."

"How do you know if you've never tried?" Karen countered.

"I have tried! My God, you think I haven't tried? I've tried my whole life to make sense of the feelings or intuition I get. It's not that easy." Lizzy felt her own exasperation from years of

15

attempting to interpret her 'feeling' data. You know I've studied and worked toward having more control over it. I wish the information was consistently clear for me but it isn't. Sometimes I'll get something loud and clear and sometimes it's like walking through mud; really stressful, annoying mud!"

"I'm sorry Lizzy. This isn't on you. I'm just freaking out and want some answers. Something or someone invaded my home!"

"I'll stay tonight and we'll see if anything occurs and go from there."

Karen had to admit she felt none of the tension from the day before. They ordered pizza and watched *Bridget Jones Diary* for at least the 10th time.

"I'm sleeping in your room tonight. You know that right?" asked Lizzy.

"Duh," Karen said with a smile.

Thankfully, Lizzy and the comic relief made her feel relaxed and normal again. Later, the two friends were finding it hard to drift off to sleep. They were both squirmed around attempting to get comfortable. They must have asked each other "What's that?" ten times. The neighbor's dog, Rudy, started barking. Both girls looked at each other in the darkened room wondering if it was animal instinct sensing some spirit wondering around or just a stray cat garnering Rudy's attention. Karen's neighbors called Rudy into the house and everything went silent. Karen and Lizzy held their breath for a moment, anxiously waiting to see if something scary would happen. When nothing out of the ordinary presented itself, they both finally drifted off to sleep.

They rolled out of bed at 6:00 a.m.

"Oddly, I slept really well," said Lizzy feeling refreshed and ready for coffee.

"Me too," said Karen.

Lizzy needed to get home. Karen's children would be home by 3:00 p.m. Lizzy was glad Karen wouldn't have to spend the night alone. Lizzy helped Karen clean up the destruction in the kitchen and hang the pictures in the living room.

"I'm out!" announced Lizzy. "Will you be ok until the kids get home?"

"Yes," said Karen. "I don't feel any of the tension I felt on Friday. Isn't that strange?"

"No, it's good," Lizzy said in relief.

Driving home, she did wonder why she hadn't noticed anything at Karen's house. She had psychic experiences her whole life, but they were impressions, words and sometimes pictures or feelings. There was a time when she was confused by her abilities and tried to push them away. In the end, that wasn't possible. She found out over the years that several family members had abilities as well. This made her feel more comfortable with what several psychics had told her were her gifts form God. She had always envied Mediums, but she certainly did not see dead people. Feeling a little envious of those who could, she wondered if someone with those gifts would have known what was going on at Karen's house.

CHAPTER 3

Karen's situation had rattled Lizzy's memory bank. Lizzy had been exposed to the paranormal at a young age. She could remember her first exposure like it was yesterday. Three little girls, two five and one six years old, sitting in a circle holding their Barbie dolls in their laps. Sheila, the oldest of the three leaned forward and whispered to her "and all the cabinet doors and windows in the house were opening and slamming closed! My mom said, 'That's it! We gotta get outta here!' and we did! We went to Aunt Paula's house that night. Mom packed the next day and we moved." Shelby was nodding in agreement clutching her doll to her chest.

"What was it?" Lizzy asked.

Sheila shrugged, "I don't know. Mom said it was a ghost."

"Like Casper?" Lizzy was now curious.

Sheila tried to explain the best she could. "It's when someone dies and then they come back but you can't always see them, but they are there. I'll tell you what though, they can be pretty noisy and scary!"

In some way, Lizzy knew what she meant and didn't like how she felt. She had not experienced death first hand. She was transfixed with Sheila's story.

"And that's not all," Shelby nudged Sheila in the side with her elbow. "Tell her about the rest."

"Well, my mom got really freaked out the other day and said she heard loud breathing in her closet. She thought it was one of us in there hiding and kept telling us to come out. We heard her calling our names so we went into the room to see what she wanted. When she saw us standing there, she started acting upset and yelled at us to leave the room. When she finally opened the closet door, no one was in there!" Sheila took a quick look around as though someone might be listening before she continued. "I heard her tell Aunt Paula that she found out a man had hung himself in there!"

Lizzy's breathing got shallow as her heart raced. She wasn't sure she knew what it meant, but didn't want to appear stupid in front of Sheila and Shelby. She messed around with the dress on her Barbie and finally got the courage to speak.

"So, there is a dead man in your mom's closet?" She felt prickly as goose bumps slid up her arms.

"You can't see him, but she hears him in there sometimes," Shelby added.

"I don't like that!" Lizzy said loudly.

"Shhhhhh! We're not supposed to tell!" Sheila shot Lizzy a dirty look and Lizzy knew to shut up. She didn't want her new friends to be mad at her.

"I never want to go in your mom's room!" Lizzy whispered.

"We won't."

That was that. The girls never went into that room, but Lizzy never forgot.

Lizzy was sure that it was that first brush with the paranormal that drove her curiosity about other dimensions, spirits and the supernatural. All her life she was drawn to stories and movies that investigated the unseen worlds she believed existed. She spent many a school night in bed with a flashlight and a book. She read *Amityville Horror* in 8th grade and couldn't sleep with the lights off for a month. After that, she tapered off on reading stories that scared her. She realized things had a heavy impact on her and that she was too sensitive to expose herself to much of the horror genre.

She was drawn to it all the same. She couldn't get enough of ghosts, big foot, angels and hauntings. If it had a supernatural twist, Lizzy wanted to know about it. Now, here she was, smack in the middle of something she had only read and heard about.

After arriving home, Lizzy grabbed her laptop and began some in-depth research. Apparently, it was quite normal for activity to come and go. Sometimes ghosts would lie dormant for 50-100 years. Sometimes a trigger, like remodeling, would cause a spirit to become active. There were stories where a type of person or family would be the trigger. Still, Karen's house was relatively new and Karen had lived in the house for two years with no occurrences. *Why would Karen suddenly start having problems now?* she wondered. She found a listing for a Paranormal Investigator who lived in the next town just a few miles away. Lizzy felt her heart begin to pound hard as she picked up the phone to call the number. Suddenly she felt silly and almost hung up, but the phone was picked up on the first ring.

The Ghost Busting Business must be slow, Lizzy chuckled to herself.

"Paranormal Investigators, this is Jeremy," the voice said on the other end of the line.

"Yes, Hello...," the words came stammering nervously out of her mouth, "I was wondering if you can tell me a little more about your group, or services, or just what it is you do."

"Essentially we attempt prove scientifically whether a location has unexplained or paranormal activity. We actually attempt to debunk any claims of a haunting. That's it in a nutshell."

"What if you can't debunk it?"

"Well, then we discuss with the home or business owners what we find. It seems to help people either way. If we are able to find an explanation for the 'spooky' things they are experiencing it often gives them relief. If we find there is activity that we can't explain it helps the client feel validated. Often times people feel they are crazy, so validating their experiences makes them feel better."

That makes sense, thought Lizzy since she saw Karen going through that exactly. "If someone has activity do you help them find a way to stop it or get it out of their house?" asked Lizzy.

"No," Jeremy said quickly.

"How is that helpful?" Lizzy was disappointed.

"We are scientists, not spiritualists. We attempt to stay neutral. If they want a clearing or a blessing we recommend they call their local Minister, Priest or Shaman."

"Do you ever use psychics?"

"Not really," said Jeremy. "We have had requests and a few people claiming to be psychic have accompanied our team, but we don't collaborate with them."

"I'm surprised by that!" said Lizzy. "It seems like you would kind of want to have a one stop shop for something like this. It's already difficult, I imagine, for someone to call you and then to find there is no real solution to their problem must cause some frustration."

"We stay neutral," Jeremy explained. "We have no desire to get mixed up in the 'religion' of anything. We have a couple of Ministers willing to do blessings for people but they prefer to only do such things for their congregational members. Are you having an issue?"

"A friend of mine just had a couple of very strange incidents happen in her home and I'm trying to help her out if I can."

Jeremy laughed and said, "So it's for a 'friend'?"

"Yes, it really is for a friend! I feel quite certain she is having a supernatural experience and if you don't have the solution to remove or clear out the problem, then I don't think you can help me," Lizzy could not hide her frustration or disappointment.

"Look," said Jeremy sensing Lizzy's annoyance. "We can't be all things to all people. The spirit realm is complex. Most people don't want to get into the thick of any religious or spiritual conflicts."

"Well that doesn't make sense to me. The whole thing is a 'spiritual issue' and not to address that head on seems ridiculous!"

"I'm sorry you see it that way Miss," said Jeremy. "Our goal is scientific. If you want to gather psychics and do cleansings and blessings maybe you should start your own group!"

"Well maybe I will!" and Lizzy hung up abruptly.

Lizzy pondered her conversation with Jeremy. She felt like she had been left dangling and if she felt that way, others probably did too. When Lizzy had an issue, she was tenacious about finding resolution. She felt even more determined to figure something out since it was for Karen. It wasn't as if she had never contemplated these kinds of issues. Years of Bible study as a teenager came rushing back. There was a lot of talk about battling darkness from the Pentecostal church she had attended. Lizzy felt a knot forming in the pit of her stomach. She remembered some of the reasons she had pulled away from her church, all churches actually. The dogma and the hypocrisy had finally become too much for her to swallow. Like a little black and white video in her head, she could see the Minister emphatically warning his parishioners of the Devil's sneaky ways to ruin good Christian's lives. The Devil may well be doing so but the constant focus on it drove Lizzy further away.

Memories came flooding back of a time period that was quite painful for Lizzy. She had pulled away years ago because the focus on the Devil became so prevalent that it began interfering with her desire to focus on what she believed to be the light of God. It was the pulling away from participating in church that was painful. Lizzy had been so conflicted about the dogma that she didn't agree with, that she had made herself sick. She wanted answers for things that the Ministers could not seem to answer. Their answers, when backed into a corner would be, "just stay away from 'that', it's of the Devil." The 'that' could be anything from a question about ghosts to why people on an island, who never heard of Christianity, were apparently going to hell. She simply could not participate further. She lost some good friends at the time. It seemed she was thinking and protecting herself from the Devil more than she was focusing on the Light and her faith in God. She had been indoctrinated for many years. She did believe there was a battle of good and evil, but preferred to focus on the positive rather than the darkness. She wasn't sure if this was some kind of battle, but the weight of the past began to rear its head.

Being clinical and scientific like Jeremy's group was not enough. Acknowledging that there was something unexplained did not fix the issue if there was a haunting or an attack. Many religious factions simply played paranormal activity off as Satan. *Is it ALL Satanic activity?* Lizzy had wondered about this as a teenager and wondered the same thing now. It seemed that many Christians, and those in the churches she had attended, subscribed to a practice of labeling anything that was paranormal or supernatural as the Occult and Satanic. She couldn't swallow that. She had many questions though, and her main concern was that Karen and the kids were safe.

Lizzy bounced around the internet and found some local psychics who claimed to have experience with hauntings, but there were not a lot of resources for blessing homes. Most websites said it was best if the homeowner did the deed. A few sites simply talked about general reluctance of most Ministers to get involved. *Really?* Lizzy thought. *What is this, a mugging in New York City and no one wants to get involved?*

Lizzy spontaneously hopped into her car and drove to a little church down the road from her house. She wanted to get some answers. A small white house had been converted into a neighborhood church. A sign on the door boldly stated "Christ's Chapel, Non-Denominational, All Are Welcomed." Lizzy heard a cynical voice pipe up in her head *yeah, yeah, yeah.*

She entered the foyer of the Church and an elderly man approached her. "Welcome," he said and reached out to shake Lizzy's hand.

"Are you the Pastor?" Lizzy asked.

"I am. You can call me Pastor Michael."

Nice. Lizzy thought, *Surely a Pastor named after an archangel will have some answers.* "I am not a member of your church but I have a question for you."

23

"Shoot," Pastor Michael said with a smile as he waved her to a sitting area in the foyer.

"My friend is having a, well a ghostly or paranormal experience at her home. I wanted to know if you might be able to do a blessing for her."

Pastor Michael's smile faded quickly. "We do blessings for our members only when requested. We don't believe in ghosts. We believe that demons may masquerade as past loved ones or a number of things. I don't think we can help you, but thank you for stopping in."

"That's it?" Lizzy gasped. The swiftness of his brush off surprised her. "It's black or white? There is no middle ground here?"

Pastor Michael shook his head as he stood up, "Correct."

Before Lizzy knew it, she was being escorted to the front doors and pushed out into the sun.

Do not cop an attitude Lizzy said to herself. Feelings from her past came rushing forward. The black and white thinking of some Christians was maddening. How can a person reach out for help and be told, by a Christian…'no help for you!' like the Soup Nazi on the Seinfeld show. This made her laugh out loud, but a heaviness settled in upon her just the same. That old feeling of rejection was creeping in. She hated that feeling. She hated feeling as if she had done something wrong but didn't know what. This whole incident at the church created cracks of insecurity that Lizzy hadn't felt for years. She sometimes felt like she didn't fit in anywhere.

CHAPTER 4

Billy and Brandi arrived home Sunday at 3:00 p.m. on the dot. Karen was elated to see them come through the door. She had gone about her day with relative ease. It was almost as though nothing strange had happened over the weekend. *Was it just the night before that the police were going through her home?* It seemed like a faded memory.

That evening the house was filled with chatter from the kids about their weekend, chores and a spaghetti dinner. Ten o'clock was lights out. Karen realized how exhausted she felt. She took a hot bath and slipped into her favorite fleece pajamas. Sleep came almost immediately.

Knock! Knock! Knock! Knock! Billy was jolted from sleep. He lay still in the silence, not sure exactly why he was awake. Knock! Knock! Knock! Three loud knocks on the wall right by his left ear sent him bolt upright and out of bed. Karen woke up with Billy crawling into her bed.

"Hello?" Karen said into the darkness.

"Mom, it's me, I want to stay in here with you tonight." Karen sat up and could see the moonlight bouncing off Billy's face. There was no mistaking that look of fear Karen saw on her boy's face.

"What's wrong Billy?"

"Something woke me up in my room. Someone was knocking on the wall!" Billy's voice escalated in pitch with his breathing now fast and shallow.

"Shhh, it's ok, I'm sure it was just a tree branch or an animal outside," Karen said as confidently as she could. "Go to sleep. We'll talk in the morning."

"I'm sleeping here," Billy said emphatically and crawled into bed with his mother. He turned over, feeling safe now next to his mother and drifted off to sleep.

Karen waited motionless in the dark until she was sure Billy was asleep. She could hear his breathing deepen. What started as fear now had had become motherly anger. Whatever she felt earlier in the house was now scaring her child.

Karen slipped out of bed and slowly edged into Billy's room. The hair on the back of her neck stood straight up as she crossed the threshold. Standing just inside the door of Billy's room she had the strangest impression of a teenage girl. A picture pressed into her mind.

That's strange, she thought. *Is that my imagination? Where is this coming from?* Karen stood still in the dark once more trying to control her breathing. She shut the door behind her careful not to alert the children and spoke sternly in a loud whisper into Billy's room.

"You can stay with us if you want, but you cannot stay if you are going to scare my children. If it continues you will have to leave," turning on her heel and stepping into the hall, Karen let her breath out quietly as she started back to her room. One loud knock sounded off in Billy's room causing her to jump.

"I'm going to assume that means you agree," she whispered into the silence. A single knock resonated from Billy's room.

Over the next couple of weeks Karen noticed small things happening in the house. None of incidents had the alarming energy of the first few occurrences. Little things disappeared and then reappeared somewhere else in the house. The makeup in her bathroom seemed to be a particular hot spot. She would find her eye shadow and mascara sitting near other mirrors throughout the house. It made getting ready for work a little taxing. Brandi noticed, what she thought was her mother, leaving her makeup scattered throughout the house.

As far as Karen could tell, her children were not being involved or disrupted further. The knocking appeared to have stopped. She felt her little talk, with what she believed to be a spirit, had worked.

Two weeks had passed without incident. She and the children played a game dominoes to end the evening.

"To bed with you two, you have school tomorrow," Karen said pushing the game to the corner of the table.

"Good night, Mom," Bradi and Billy said in unison, kissing their mother goodnight and shuffling to their bedrooms. Karen read her newest romance novel briefly and turned out the light. Just as she was falling asleep, the distinct sound of a domino tapping on the dining room table filled her room. She could not believe they would sneak back out to play. She went quietly to the kitchen expecting to catch Billy and Brandi in the act. The dining room light was on but the children were nowhere to be found. Turning off the light she slipped back into bed hoping to fall asleep quickly. Then, out of the silence she could hear the domino tapping the table.

"Go to sleep!" she said into the darkness and it stopped. This game went on for the next three nights. The third night Karen put the game away but was roused from sleep an hour later by the same sound emanating from the dining room.

"Seriously, go to sleep now!" she said out load from her bed. The tapping once again stopped.

Lizzy called with her findings on house cleansing but Karen felt she had solved the issue with her 'little talk' to the spirit.

"Why do you think it is a teenage girl?" asked Lizzy.

"I just got a heavy impression. It was like a picture of an adolescent girl and brief moment of her feelings were pressed into my mind. It's kind of hard to explain," said Karen.

"I think I understand. I've had that happen to me. Maybe not exactly but a version of getting information and having it pressed into me. "You are sure you're not scared?" asked Lizzy.

"No, I'm not right now. So far I think she has backed off."

"I just don't get it," Lizzy pressed. "Where did she come from and why is she there?"

"I don't know Lizzy. I feel kind of bad for her. That's why I said she could stay as long as she behaved herself."

"Ok, I guess we'll keep an eye on it but I've read that things can escalate without warning. I would prefer to bless the house and try and get her out of there!" Lizzy was not comfortable with Karen's decision to leave the spirit in her home.

"Lizzy, I'm ok. I'm going to let her stay."

Brandi's friend Tina had graduated a year ahead of Brandi. Tina's mother was rarely home while Tina was growing up. She absolutely could not be without a man. She would morph into whatever person the man she was dating wanted. She would often act as though she didn't have a daughter at home waiting for her. There were dramatic fights between her and Tina. Tina often took refuge at Karen's house. It was no wonder that she had always been insecure. As a teenager, she created situations to gain attention, but Karen knew she was a good-hearted girl. Karen heard a knock at the door and for a moment thought *Oh no, not again!* She was relieved when she opened the door to find Tina on the other side of it.

"You're just in time for dinner," Karen chirped.

Tina made her way into the house and plopped down on the couch.

"So, how have you been?" asked Karen. Tina sighed deeply and began telling Karen all about one of her professors she thought was hitting on her.

"He's married you know," Tina added at the end of her story.

. "If this continues I think you should report him," Karen said sternly. What kind of man hits on an 18 year old girl in his class?

"I don't know that I want to do that!" shrieked Tina.

"Well, are you encouraging him Tina?" Tina sat silently. "Tina, you need to stay focused on school and stop creating drama for yourself. You're just replaying your childhood and creating drama where you don't need it. You know I'm right!" Karen's brow furrowed and Tina knew she needed to stop stirring the pot.

Tina had always considered Karen her honorary mother. Karen was the mother she wished she had. Her relationship with her own mother was still tense at best. She was sure her mother didn't really like her and the feeling was mutual. Tina spent many a warm night at Karen's with Brandi. There were times that her jealousy got the best of her and she would find herself snapping at Brandi for no reason. Over the years, Karen had given her a lot of support. Karen was no pushover and Tina knew it. She also knew that Karen would call Tina out if she were creating unnecessary havoc in her own life. Karen would not tolerate Tina pulling Brandi into anything that would get her into trouble. She had grown to need Karen's approval, and would not do anything to jeopardize the relationship.

She had benefited from Karen's firm loving hand during her turbulent teenage years. Now at the tender age of 19, she felt she still needed Karen's consistent nature in her life. It soothed her and helped her feel safe.

Tina loved the warm energy of Karen's house. It always smelled like spiced apple pie from scented candles.   Karen specialized in the best comfort food in the world and Tina learned to coordinate her visits with dinnertime. Tonight was no exception. She could smell the pot roast simmering in the oven.

Tina noticed something different when she stepped into the house. She couldn't quite put her finger on it. As she was washing her hands in the bathroom, she couldn't shake the feeling that someone was watching her. There was a light "knock, knock knock" at the bathroom door. She opened it expecting to see Brandi but there was no one. As she entered the kitchen, Brandi and Billy were sitting at the counter talking to Karen. *That's weird*, she thought.

Karen looked up from the pot of potatoes she was mashing and said, "Nice timing, we're having your favorite." A big smile crossed Karen's face.

"What can I do to help?"

Karen's head snapped over to Brandi and Billy at the counter and rolled her eyes, "How about all of you get the table set."

Brandi smirked at Tina, "Brown noser!" Tina smiled as they set the table, she knew she was and didn't care.

Tina began to ramble about school, her job and the most recent calamity with her mother. She decided to side step further conversations about the professor since Billy was present.

Karen patted her on the back, "Just stay positive and keep moving forward, Tina. Remember, the past does not equal the future. You are the one in the driver's seat now. You can make good choices, or choices that create chaos in your life. You are not your mother! I know you will do great things in the future if you just keep that in mind."

Tina knew this was sound advice. It was hard to follow sometimes. Her immediate support system was limited to Brandi and Karen. Her mother was in Mexico with some guy she met two weeks prior. Tina was sure she would come home with a Mexican marriage certificate.

Tina lived an hour north near the college in Sand Hollow. Her apartment was in an old house that had been converted into a triplex for students. Her neighbor upstairs was Anna, a quiet Biology student. They passed in the foyer occasionally but were not personally acquainted with each other. Her neighbor with a connecting wall was a husky football player named Greg. He had always been very nice. All of them seemed to live harmoniously. Occasionally, Greg would have some of the boys over and it would get a little loud but never past 10:00 pm. When she had first moved in, Greg invited her over for a bar-b-que. There had never been any issues between the three of them and Tina was happy for that bit of peace in her life.

"Alright," Tina piped up, "I've got to get going. Thank you again for dinner, Karen!"

"Any time Tina. Keep studying and stay focused on your school work not that professor!"

"I will," Tina promised. She and Brandi walked to the door, hugged and she departed.

The warm air on her face felt good as she walked to her car. Tina opened the door and a chill ran up her spine. *That's weird,* she thought. A creepy feeling suddenly gripped her. She spun around to check the back seat, half expecting someone to be there. *Empty of course*, she thought. She began her hour trek home feeling grateful for the kindness Brandi and her family had shown her all these years. She flicked the radio on to her favorite country station and let her mind wander. Her radio dimmed and switched stations. Without thinking too much about it she switched it back and began singing along. Again, the radio dimmed and switched stations. It went to 106.7, the 80's Wave, a station she hated.

"What is going on?" she said aloud as she switched it back. Five minutes later the radio dimmed and the station skipped into "Girls just want to have fun" on 106.7 the 80's Wave.

She switched the station back. This had never happened to her before. She wondered if she had an electrical problem that she would need to fix. This was something she really didn't want to entertain due to her tight budget.

The aroma of a sweet powdery perfume filled the car. She rolled her window down, confused, she decided to turn the radio off completely in case there was an electrical problem. The radio immediately came back on. The hair rose on the back of Tina's neck and she felt a little dizzy. The odor was overwhelming. She pressed her foot on the accelerator, wanting to get home and out of her car as soon as possible. It was a long 40 minutes of 80's retro and stinking perfume. Tina pulled into her parking spot a little too fast and gravel and dust sprayed up as she stopped. She quickly gathered her things out of the back seat and jumped the three steps

31

to the porch. *Get a grip,* she thought, *you are overreacting.* She couldn't shake the feeling that someone had been with her in the car.

CHAPTER 5

Three weeks after Tina's visit, Karen relaxed reading her favorite magazine.

Billy rushed through the door yelling, "Mom! Mom! Mom!"

"You scared me! "

Winded, Billy rushed to his mother and started talking so fast she could barely understand him.

"Sorry Mom, but I was just talking to Ben and Sara down the street and Ben said they had a ghost, a girl, a ghost girl in their house!"

Karen cut him off, "Slow down Billy, catch your breath! Now continue, calmly."

Billy took a couple of deep, strained breaths and started over. "Ben and I were talking and Ben told me that they have, or had, a ghost in their house. Ben said he saw her once, it was a girl…a teenage girl. Sara said that she used to bang on the walls at night and scare the crap out of them. Ben said he didn't know where she came from but about a month ago, things stopped! He said his family was finally sleeping through the night. And now I want to know, do you think she is here, with us now?"

Karen felt sick to her stomach. Why would he think that? The furniture and water incident happened while the kids were at their father's house and Billy never brought up the knocking incident after that one night he had stayed in her room. *If there is a spirit,* she thought, *she had backed it down. Hadn't she? There hadn't been any further incidents, had there?*

"Billy, why would you ask that?"

Billy started slowly, "Well, because…" he stopped cold. She was going to think he was crazy or a baby.

"Billy, tell me why!" Karen raised her voice to get his attention.

"Well, remember the night I stayed in your room because of the knocking?"

Karen nodded.

"Well," Billy stopped to think for a moment if he should go on. "I think there has been a girl in my room since then!"

Karen's heart began to pound hard through her chest and an immediate feeling of defeat swept through her. She thought she had put that to rest, put her to rest. She thought they had an agreement; she could stay as long as she didn't scare the children.

"Billy, why would you think there was a girl in your room?" Karen said as calmly as she could.

"Well, ever since that night I have just felt like someone was watching me in my room. Sometimes there is a smell, a perfume smell like, well kind of like sweet baby powder. And, she knocks on the wall when I'm sleeping and I have heard her say my name," Billy said, now looking at the floor in embarrassment.

"How often are you hearing knocking on the walls, Billy?" Karen asked still trying to appear calm.

"Oh, mom, pretty much every night. If I go into my room and smell that perfume, I know she's there and probably going to bug me all night."

"What!" Karen was taken completely off guard by this information. "Why didn't you say something to me, Billy?"

"I don't know. I didn't know what to say. I tried to tell Brandi and she told me to shut up. I wasn't sure you'd believe me and I don't want you to think I'm being a baby!"

"I would never think something like that, Billy! If anything like this ever happens again or you are afraid for any reason, you need to come to me." Karen was holding back her tears. She was a complete failure as a mother as far as she was concerned. She had to take care of this situation immediately!

Ben and Sara were older than Billy. They didn't hang out generally, but now Karen was wondering if they had been in the house.

"Billy, did you have Ben or Sara over here at all last month?" Karen asked nervously.

Billy paused and thought about it. "Yes, Ben came over to collect for the paper. Remember, you left me the money to give to him. I did take him to my room to show him my new 'Rant' video game." Billy could see now where his mother was going with her question. "Oh man, Mom…Mom…do you think she's in our house now? Is it my fault because I had him in my room? Do you think she came in with Ben? That's so creepy!" Billy's eyes were as big as saucers.

Karen, now mortified couldn't believe this had been happening. Poor sleep-deprived Billy! He had been dealing with this and had never said a word!

"Billy, I don't know what has happened here. I am so sorry she scared you. I had no idea you were being bothered. I wish you would have said something!" Karen grabbed her son and hugged him tight.

"Mom," said Billy as he wriggled away, "I wasn't exactly scared. I didn't know what was happening at first. Maybe I didn't even totally realize it until just now when Ben told me his story. I mean, I've been uncomfortable but I wasn't exactly scared. Okay, the night I heard knocking right by my head, that night I was scared. When I heard her call my name, at first I thought it was Brandi so it didn't frighten me. After I realized it wasn't Brandi I felt funny for sure. She did quit knocking by my head and did

35

most of it on the other side of the room. It's more like a creepy, cold feeling in my room and around the house, like I'm being watched. I don't like that. Things have been moved in my room and I know I didn't move them. Anyway, when Ben told me his story I just sort of freaked out and thought I should tell you. So, Mom, what do you think we should do?"

Karen sat in silence for a moment, "I don't know. The next time you notice something I want you to tell me right away." Billy nodded in approval. "Has Brandi said anything about any of this?"

"We talked about it awhile back. She smelled the perfume in my room. She told me that some of her makeup went missing and then she found it in her closet stacked on the floor. She blamed me but I didn't do it!"

Karen patted Billy on the back. "Just let me know the next time you notice something Billy. I will talk to your sister."

Brandi got home just before dinner. Karen followed her to her room and related what Billy had told her.

Brandi shrugged somewhat unsurprised. "I have felt it. I smelled something in Billy's room once when he insisted I come check it out. I didn't know if he was just messing with me but he seemed serious. After my makeup went missing, I told her and Billy both to stay out of my room. I never felt it in there again."

"When is the last time you noticed anything?" asked Karen.

Brandi thought for a moment before answering, "I'm not sure, but I haven't noticed anything for about a week or so. "

"If you notice anything Brandi, I need you need to tell me immediately. If your brother comes to you with any concern you need to tell me," instructed Karen.

"Fine, fine," Brandi said as she waved her mother off and went on unloading her books from her backpack. Brandi hated any kind of drama or upheaval. She was well-grounded and refused to get caught up in the excitement. If there was a ghost, it wasn't bothering her and she wanted to keep it that way.

36

Karen finished dinner wondering the whole time if they had an unseen guest for dinner.

CHAPTER 6

Lizzy hadn't heard from Karen in week, which was a little unusual so she stopped by on her way home from work. Karen broke out one of her favorite bottles of wine and asked Lizzy to stay for a glass. As Karen poured the wine, Lizzy impatiently asked, "Well? What's the news? I haven't heard from you in a week. What's going on?"

Lizzy noticed the drained look on Karen's face as she sat down at the kitchen table. Karen related the events of the evening.

"Lizzy, I thought nothing like what went on a few weeks ago had happened again, except the knocking incident where Billy came to my room. At least, I thought that was the last thing that happened, but apparently, there have been other things happening that Billy didn't tell me about until today. I feel really guilty."

"Why are you feeling guilty?" Lizzy asked, puzzled.

"Why wouldn't I? Some spirit has been tormenting my children for almost a month. Billy has had virtually no sleep this last month because I didn't protect him. I don't know what to do."

"Look," said Lizzy, "this is not your fault. I mean how you can even think you could anticipate any of this, let alone know what to do is crazy talk. You thought you had made an agreement with her, but apparently she pushed the limits. Sounds just like a teenage girl, doesn't it?"

"Yes it does, but I was very firm."

"Ooooooooooooh you were firm! That would do it I guess."

Karen was not amused with Lizzy's sarcasm. "Lizzy, I can't have something bothering the kids."

Lizzy agreed no one should have to be afraid, or feel creepy in their home, especially children. "I'm just glad Billy came to you. I'm sure that wasn't easy. Maybe we can find some more information out about this girl and cleanse the house."

"I don't even know what that entails," snapped Karen.

"I've been researching it online since all this began. There is a plethora of paranormal information out there. Apparently, you aren't the only one plagued with a spirit or ghost. It seems pretty rampant out there." Lizzy paused and grabbed her purse. "Here, this is a house blessing I found online." She pulled a bundle of white pages out of her purse and slid it across the table to Karen. "This is supposed to help clear out spirits from a home."

"What, you just carry this stuff in your purse now?"

"Karen, I've wanted to do a blessing since the start. You know I was never comfortable you leaving her to stay in the house with you. I don't know why I didn't feel good about it. I know there are other people online who have done just what you did and live happily with their ghostly friends. I just didn't feel good about this from the beginning."

"Right, exactly my point," Karen said wiping a tear from the corner of her eye. "I'm a horrible mother. I should have done the blessing from the beginning."

"Oh stop!" Lizzy got up from the table and hugged her friend's shoulders. "It isn't like this is an everyday occurrence that everyone knows how to handle. It's not as if you were chasing a dog out of your yard. You are dealing with the spirit world! If we knew everything about it, no one would be afraid to die. We'd just know we could hook up with our dead relatives and make the call when we needed them. This is not part of our everyday lives. Please quit beating yourself up! It hasn't even been a full month. Some people endure hauntings for years. Many are far more sinister than this."

"Okay, fine I'm not doing this by myself you know!" said Karen. "You're the one who's the Minister-Psychic, maybe you should do the blessing."

Lizzy had been ordained twice. Once, after a Hypnotherapy Certification Course 10 years prior and again two years ago when she took an Ordination Class from her spiritual mentor, Teresa. Yes, she was an ordained minister; however, she had only used it to perform wedding ceremonies over the years. She never thought of herself as an actual minister but the truth was she was a minister and denial wasn't changing that fact.

"I'm not doing it by myself, either," Lizzy protested. "We can do it together. Really, it is very important that you participate since it is your house. I'll come over tomorrow after work if that works for you and we'll do the deal!"

"Fine," said Karen and they shook on it.

Lizzy's curiosity was getting the best of her and she did a little more research to see if she could find out more about the "girl down the street." *Who was she? How did she end up in Karen's house if she had been in Ben and Sara's house?* she asked herself. Although she had been intrigued since childhood with the paranormal, Lizzy had never had many direct experiences. She had feelings, hunches and sometimes got information from out of nowhere but to have an actual "ghostly" encounter had never happened. She wasn't sure if she was envious or relieved. She wasn't sure where to start. It seemed logical to start at Ben and Sarah's and talk to their parents.

She had crossed paths only once with Ben's father, Justin Blake. He worked at the Greenhurst National Bank and had ordered some promotional pens and key chains from her. *How is this going to go over?* she asked herself imaging the worst. *Hi Justin, just wanted to talk to you about the spirit haunting your kids. She seems to be down the block haunting my friend now...*

She sat in her car in front of the Blake's house for a few minutes before getting the courage to approach the door. She pushed the button, the doorbell had a happy chime and she heard footsteps approaching the door. Justin opened the door and was noticeably surprised to see Lizzy standing on the other side.

"Well, hello," he said, "what brings you here? We paid you for the key chains didn't we?"

"Oh my gosh, yes! This is about another matter completely," said Lizzy, hoping he wouldn't throw her off the stoop once she started talking. "Mr. Blake, this is going to sound strange but could you step outside with me for a moment? I have a couple questions for you if you will indulge me."

Mr. Blake stepped out onto the porch and immediately crossed his arms over his chest. "What is it Ms. Sterling?"

Lizzy began, "My friend Karen lives a couple blocks over. Her son Billy knows your son Ben. Billy was talking to Ben today and, well, Ben told him that you've had a little trouble with…" she trailed off, as Mr. Blake's face seemed to harden the longer she spoke. "Ben said you have had a haunting." There, she got it out, quick like ripping off a band-aid.

"And? What? You want to write a story or something? What do you want Lizzy?" Obviously taken off guard, Mr. Blake took another step back from Lizzy but wasn't denying what Ben had said.

"No, I don't want to write a story! As strange as this may sound, my friend Karen began having some paranormal type issues about a month ago, after Ben collected for his paper route. Billy had invited him in to see a video game. After that, Karen began experiencing knocking on the walls, furniture moving and water being turned on and, well a variety of things."

"What does this have to do with me?" asked Mr. Blake.

"Ben said your house has been pretty peaceful for about a month."

Justin just stared back at Lizzy and said nothing.

"Look, I'm not going to publish this on the front page of the paper. I'm just trying to help Karen and I thought you might be able to give me some insight. Whatever it is has been scaring her son for the last month and she's sick about it," Lizzy couldn't believe he was stonewalling her.

Mr. Blake relax a little. "Lizzy, I don't want this getting around town. I'm already upset that Ben told Billy. I manage a bank. What are people going to think if I say my house is haunted? Do you understand? I don't want to talk about this."

"Please just answer a few questions and I'll leave. I will not talk to anyone about what you've told me. In fact, if I hear anyone talk about your house I will tell them it was a mistake and that it was Karen's house with the problem. With your houses in the same neighborhood, I'm sure it will be easily passed off. Please Justin."

He lowered his arms to his side. "All right, what do you want to know?"

"How long has it been going on?" she asked.

"Since we moved in, about a year and a half ago."

"Did anyone in the family ever feel it was a young girl?" Lizzy inquired further.

He looked a little surprised before cautiously answering, "Yes. We all got that impression at one time or another. My son said he actually saw her. We would smell a perfume throughout the house sometimes. It was mostly centered around Ben. My wife is at her wits end about the whole thing. We have been talking about moving. Ben has been affected the most and the kid has taken it all pretty well, but we decided about two months ago that we should probably look for another place to live."

"I'd wait on that if I were you," Lizzy said with a sigh.

"Why?"

"I honestly think she has moved over to Karen's house. I don't know how exactly but she did. Ben told Billy things have been quiet for about a month here. For the last month, things have not been quiet for Billy. He seems to be experiencing all the same things Ben did. If I were you, I would wait a little bit and see if you are still having any more issues. If not, then maybe you won't have to move after all."

Justin looked relieved. "I don't know if I believe it. We've been battling this for over a year now. To think it is over is kind of weird but welcomed."

"I know," said Lizzy empathetically. "I think she has left your residence. It is too coincidental that Billy would be experiencing the exact same thing as Ben, in my opinion."

"I'm sorry for Karen," Justin said sadly. "I don't wish this upon anyone!"

"So, other than what you've told me, can you think of any reason this might have been happening here?" asked Lizzy.

"No, I don't. We've never had anything like this happen to us and I hope to never have another brush with it in the future," Justin said rubbing his forehead.

"Thank you Justin, I appreciate your help. I hope this won't affect our business relationship."

"It won't. Just make sure you get me another order in the next month," Justin said now smiling.

"Will do," said Lizzy.

That was stressful! It was interesting though, she thought as she started her engine and headed for home.

Monday, Lizzy couldn't concentrate on work. Racking her brain, she was thinking who might be able to help her. Then she remembered Mary Johnson. Mary had lived in that neighborhood for 40 years. She was also a bit of a busybody so Lizzy thought it might be a good idea to check it out. If Mary hadn't heard any scuttlebutt, then no one had. Lizzy decided to skip lunch and see if Mary was home.

The gravel crunched beneath Lizzy's feet as she neared Mary's door. *This is probably going to sound crazy. How am I going to broach this with Mary without sounding nuts?* Too late, her finger already pressed the doorbell and she could hear footsteps shuffling toward her. As the door swung open, there was Mary with a big smile on her face. "Lizzy Sterling what in the world are you doing here? I haven't seen you in what, five years?"

"Hello Mary, I am thoroughly ashamed of myself for being so scarce, how are you?" Mary motioned Lizzy through the door.

"Just dandy Lizzy. I've been just dandy. What can I do you for missy?"

Mary was short, hobbit short. She was as round as she was tall and one of the most pleasant people Lizzy had ever known. Mary volunteered at the Elementary school and for various events around town. Lizzy had met her when she was in the third grade at some Memorial Day event at the local park. Later she saw her often at the school. Throughout high school, she would drop by every now and then to visit with Mary and her husband Hank. Hank was a robust man with a big laugh. He liked to tease Lizzy and always gave her a big bear hug when she came around. Hank had passed away five years prior. Lizzy realized that she had stopped in on Mary that first year and then got caught up in her own life and sort of drifted away. Mary filled her time with grandchildren and the "Red Hat Ladies" events. When Lizzy thought back, the only time she ever remembered seeing Mary without a broad smile on her face was at her husband's funeral. That was a sad day indeed. Mary seemed to have bounced back and here she was looking healthy and happy.

"Mary, I need a little help with something and I am hoping you won't think I'm nuts."

"Oh pshaw!" with that, Mary jumped up and went toward the kitchen. "How about some iced tea?"

"Sure," Lizzy called behind her. The house smelled of lilacs and roses. Mary had a large wedding picture of her and Hank hanging over the mantel. Mary once had quite the hourglass figure in her 20's. Small pictures of children and grandchildren were scattered on the mantel and tables.

Mary handed Lizzy an iced tea and plopped into the wing-backed chair across from her. She was spry for a round woman in her 60's.

44

"Mary, I was wondering do you know of any teenage girls who passed away over in the Sycamore neighborhood?"

Mary looked surprised and her bright smile faded, which worried Lizzy. "Why do you ask child?"

"I will tell you, but before I reveal my full lunacy, I'd appreciate any information you might have."

Mary drew a deep breath and began, "Her name was Sunday, Sunday Stewart. Her family moved over there on Oak and Second in about 1990.

"Where Justin Blake and his family live now?"

Mary nodded.

"So, she was about 15 I think, maybe 16. I think she was a sophomore. She was a nice little gal. They belonged to my church. They were a nice enough family. They had a young boy as well, he was a little younger than Sunday. Unfortunately he was the one who found her."

"Found her?" Lizzy repeated.

"John and Silvia, her parents, worked a lot. They were both on the fast tracks at their jobs. Sunday got herself hooked up with a boy, I won't say who. Apparently, they had gotten serious, at least Sunday thought they were on the road to marriage. You know, teenage girls," Mary paused and shook her head in disbelief, "sometimes they make more of love or the act of love than it really is."

"So, what happened?" Lizzy pleaded.

"The boy left for college and got engaged to another girl. He failed to inform Sunday. She found out when the engagement announcement came out in the paper. She was crushed. She solved her grief by taking every pill she found in her parent's medicine cabinet. The cocktail was enough to kill her. She left a note that simply said 'I hope they're happy in hell.' Her little brother came home from school and found her on the couch, dead."

Lizzy and Mary sat in silence for a few moments. "Why do you ask Lizzy?" Mary said finally.

"Mary, Ben Blake told Karen's son Billy that they thought a spirit had been haunting their house, a spirit of a teenage girl. She would bang on the walls and scare them half to death. About three weeks ago, Karen had several strange incidents at her home. She has lived there for over two years and has never had any issues or strange happenings. All of a sudden, she has water turning on and furniture moving and knocking on the walls. Apparently, Ben told Billy his story and Billy was experiencing the exact same things. Billy put two and two together and thought maybe she had somehow come to his house," Lizzy waited for Mary to toss her out on her ear.

Mary didn't seem entirely surprised. "Lizzy, I've heard some things about that house the Blake's live in over the years. You know, people don't talk about that kind of stuff very often but occasionally something slips out. I'm not surprised, although I don't know why in the world Karen would experience anything. Doesn't she live a few streets over?"

"She does," said Lizzy, "but what she is experiencing is very similar to what Ben said was going on at their house. Ben had been in Billy's room about three weeks ago. He was collecting his paper route money and Billy took him inside to show him a video game. The only thing I can figure is the ghost somehow had attached to Ben and moved over to Karen's," Lizzy now realized she sounded ridiculous.

"I don't know about any of that Lizzy," said Mary, "but it was a sad situation all around. I feel bad for the families who have lived in that house because I don't think Sunday's spirit has been at peace."

Lizzy decided to change the subject and asked Mary about her grandchildren. This brought the usual big smile back to Mary's round face. The rest of the visit went well and Lizzy was happy that they reconnected. She promised herself and Mary she wouldn't be so scarce in the future.

"I've got to get back to work Mary, thank you for your help and the tea," and with that Lizzy was out the door.

CHAPTER 7

Karen waited nervously for Lizzy to arrive to begin the house blessing. She hoped it would work, although she had not felt a presence or noticed anything strange for a week. Things had been quiet. She took the children to their father's house for the night. Karen jumped when Lizzy knocked on the door. Lizzy stepped into the living room and gently put her bag on the floor.

"What is all this?" Karen said, pointing to the bag.

"I had to stop and get some stuff for the blessing." One by one, she brought out the tools of the trade.

1 Bible
1 white candle in a tall glass jar
1 bundle of White Sage
1 bottle of Holy Water
1 bottle of Sandalwood Anointing Oil
1 bag of Sea Salt

"Wow," said Karen, "what do we do with all this?"

"As you know, I'm no expert. I did some research online and talked to the Minister who taught the Ordination Class. I think I understand what to do to cleanse, bless and protect the house but you do need to participate."

"I'm right here, Lizzy," said Karen. "just tell me what you want me to do."

"Before we start, we need to talk about what I found out from Mary Johnson today."

"Mary Johnson?" Karen laughed, "what does that busybody have to do with anything?"

"Hey, don't act like that. She was very helpful today. Sometimes being a busybody and being a friend of a busybody has its advantages. One advantage being she knows just about everything that's happened in this town in the last 40 years. She is a nice woman," Lizzy said a little disgruntled.

"Ok already, Mary Johnson, Queen of the Universe then! What did she have to say?" Karen couldn't stop smirking.

"A teenage girl, Sunday Stewart killed herself in Ben's house in the 90s. I think she may be the spirit who has been in your house. I don't know how she got here, but it all just sort of adds up. She had a little brother, Josh, who found her."

"That's horrible," said Karen. "I've never heard of any of this."

"Well," Lizzy continued, "Mary Johnson had. Anyway, I think Sunday has been lingering around. She was a jilted lover and downed a bunch of pills. You know teenage angst."

"I think she hitched a ride over here, but why and how?" asked Karen.

"I don't know," said Lizzy, "but if she did, we will attempt to usher her out. We need to open the back and front door. The instructions I read say to start in the living room of the house and begin working clockwise into every room and closet. You carry the candle and sprinkle holy water around and I'll deal with burning the sage and putting crosses on the door casings with the oil. It says to put a cross on every doorway and window casing with the oil, while stating the prayer. I printed a copy for you. I feel kind of bad casting her out though. I don't know if maybe we can direct her to the light. I just don't know. I am feeling a little inept."

If Lizzy was feeling inept, Karen was feeling completely out of her universe. The two women took a moment to say a prayer at the table and then moved all the gear into the living room. Lizzy lit the candle and handed it to Karen. Lighting a small part of the sage bundle, Lizzy let it burn for a minute and then blew it out creating a steady plume of smoke. She opened the Bible, pushed the small bottle of oil into her pocket and placed her copy of the prayer into the middle of the Bible. She began to read with a firm loud voice from Ephesians 6:10-17 for protection and blessing.

Slowly they moved clockwise through the house, and in unison, read the prayer in each room.

"We consecrate this room in the name of God through our Lord Jesus Christ. As the smoke from this Sage rises so do our prayers to the ear of God. The light of this candle burns away all negative energies or spirits in this home. We command any negative spirit in this room to depart and never return."

Lizzy added, "If you can hear me Sunday Stewart, look for the light and move toward it. You have passed and are in limbo. Go toward the light if you can see or sense it."

Karen sprinkled the holy water as she followed Lizzy. Lizzy demanded, "We consecrate this room and this house in the name of God the Father, God the Mother, Jesus and in the name of the Holy Spirit, Amen."

They winded their way through the whole house and ended in the living room where they started and said the following prayer together:

"Lord we commit this house to you today, if any wrongs have been done to bring this upon this house or this family we ask forgiveness. If any spirit is lost and seeking the light we ask that you and the angels lead the way to peace for these spirits. We ask you to call angels to guard this house as we now commit it to you Dear Father. Guard Karen, Brandi and Billy. Protect those who enter this house. This family is now consecrated and freely given to you God, and now we put our trust and confidence in you to protect us, in the name of Jesus, Amen."

Lizzy motioned for Karen to follow her outside. She then sprinkled salt in front of each door and began walking in a circle clockwise around the property sprinkling the salt in a protective circle.

The two friends walked with a lighter skip in their feeling something had lifted.

"Thank you Lizzy." Karen said as she hugged her friend.

Lizzy felt the faint buzz pulsing through her body that she always felt after working with energy. She was feeling very revved up. Lizzy felt this same vibrational buzz in her Ordination class when learning Reiki. *It must be a good sign that the energy is moving more freely and in a positive way,* she thought.

"Do you think God would mind if we had a glass of wine?" Karen asked sheepishly.

"I don't think so, let's have a toast to a blessed house!"

CHAPTER 8

The three weeks that passed since Tina had visited Brandi left her feeling unbalanced. So many strange things had been going on she thought maybe she was going crazy. At one point she really had thought she might be certifiable. Fortunately did find out that she was not the only one experiencing strange occurrences.

The wall knocking started the night after she arrived home. At first, she thought it was Greg. *Why would he do that?* She tried to ignore it. Then she heard Anna moving furniture around at all hours of the night. This went on for three weeks when finally on Sunday she heard a loud knock on her door. She opened the door to find Greg standing on the other side. He had a scowl on his face normally smiling face. "Hi Greg," she said, "what's up?"

"What's up with you?" he was obviously annoyed.

Tina stood there for a moment not knowing what to do, and then motioned for Greg to come in. He had been in her apartment before and made his way to the couch. She noticed he looked tired.

"Greg, what is it?"

"Tina, what have you been doing over here? I've heard you knocking on the wall and I don't know if you and Anna have some kind of furniture moving pact but I can hear you two moving furniture at all hours of the night! If it's not you, it's her. You know, we've all gotten on pretty well here together but I've got to get some sleep!"

"I am not knocking on the wall and I haven't moved my furniture around either as you can plainly see!" Tina felt embarrassed but wasn't sure why.

"Tina, I can hear you! How can you tell me it isn't you?"

"Well, it isn't. I thought it was you. I've been hearing furniture moving in Anna's apartment and I've heard the wall knocking but I thought it was you. I didn't know what to think."

This answer clearly was not satisfying Greg. "I'm tired Tina, I haven't slept in three weeks and I'm just asking you to stop."

"It isn't me, Greg, I swear!"

As the two students sat in silence and pondered the other's nocturnal behavior, four loud knocks sounded off on the wall between Tina and Greg's apartments.

Tina and Greg gasped and stared at the wall. "Is someone in your apartment Greg?" Tina asked.

He shook his head, leapt to his feet and sprinted out the door to his apartment. Tina followed him, a little surprised at how quickly such a big guy could move! Greg's apartment was a small one bedroom with an open kitchen and living area similar to Tina's apartment. He checked the bedroom, looked under the bed and then the bathroom.

"There is no one here," he said confused. Tina was just about to say they should check with Anna when four loud knocks came through the wall from her apartment.

Greg's mouth dropped open. Tina took a couple steps back.

"What was going on?" Tina yelled.

"I have no idea," said Greg.

"Maybe we should talk to Anna and see if she has noticed anything," suggested Tina.

"I'll see if she's home," said Greg. He moved quickly toward the foyer stairs.

"I'm coming with you," said Tina realizing she didn't want to be alone and shadowed him up the stairs to Anna's apartment. Both started knocking on Anna's. Tina pulled her fist away from the door just as Anna opened it.   Anna took a step and was obviously not excited by her visitors.

"Can I help you?" Anna said with a little bit of a growl in her voice.

Tina and Greg seized up. They stood mouths shut staring at Anna.   Anna stood unmoved at the door and stared back. Tina finally broke the standoff by blurting out, "have you been moving your furniture around at night?"

"What? Really? With all the banging around you two have been doing down there you have the nerve to come up here with that?"

"That's WHY we are here. Anna, please come downstairs. We have something to talk to you about," said Tina.

"Why should I?" said Anna. "I don't know you two and quite honestly I'm a little pissed!"

"Look Anna," Tina began to explain, "we've all been hearing the same things but none of us are the ones doing it."

"What ARE you talking about?" Anna pushed her wire rim glasses back, crossed her arms and took a stern stance with Tina and Greg. Anna's petite stature seemed bigger in the doorway some how. Tina took a step back and tried to avoid the glare Anna was sending her.

"Either come down to my apartment or let us in so we can talk to you!" Tina felt her chest begin to tighten as her anxiety grew. It was clear to her that neither Anna nor Greg had been creating the noise she had been hearing.

Anna took another look at Greg, who was still silent, but obviously shook up about something. His eyes were darting back and forth wildly. "All right, come in. Greg, are you ok?" Anna said letting her guard down a little.

Greg rubbed the side of his face as if he'd just been smacked.

"To be honest, I'm completely freaked out."

Tina and Greg followed Anna into her apartment. It was almost twice the size of Greg and Tina's apartments. She had a fireplace in her living area and the light streamed in the windows that wrapped completely around living area. The ceilings were high with an ornate header that went around the room. It was definitely the nicest of the three apartments. Putting her envy aside, Tina sat down on the edge of the couch while Greg went to the window and stared out over the back yard.

"Anna," Tina started again, "we are all hearing the same thing but none of us are making the noises! Greg was just in my apartment asking me the same thing when we heard three knocks on the wall coming from his apartment. No one is there. While we were in his apartment checking to see what it was, three knocks came through the wall from my apartment! Anna, no one was there, so now we are here."

"So, what? Are you implying that we have a ghost?" Anna said incredulously.

"Basically, yes," said Tina.

Greg piped up from the window, "This is crazy!"

"Well, as crazy as it sounds, I can't find other way to explain what's been happening."

"What do we do now?" Anna asked. "Does any one want a beer or a glass of wine?

"Beer,thanks," Greg said without moving.

Tina felt a twinge of guilt. *Had whatever had been in my car three weeks ago come into the apartments? Was this my fault?* She decided not to expand on the story.

"I'll call my friend. She's like my second mom and see if she knows what we can do."

"I'm not staying here," Greg said, turning around, his face ash white.

"Really?" said Tina. "You're going to leave us here alone?"

"What can I do?" Greg said, trying to make himself feel better about leaving.

"Look, we're all in this together. We're all hearing it and there's no guarantee that whatever it is won't follow us," Tina pointed out.

"Why would you say something like that?" yelled Greg as storm now crossing his face.

"Calm down Greg!" Anna jumped to Tina's defense. "Tina is right. We've never had trouble before and now we are, so something has changed." Anna's scientific mind was working in high gear now. None of this made sense.

Anna kept a cool detached position and appeared to be the most calm of the three. Greg started pacing and seemed seemed like he'd be climbing the walls any minute. Tina contemplated the situation and held her anxiety in check.

"We've been dealing with this for a few weeks. It doesn't appear to be harmful, so let's check around and see what we can find out about getting this thing out of here." Anna spoke authoritatively for such a quiet petite little thing. They all agreed that as long as nothing harmful occurred they could handle a little noise. They agreed to stay in Anna's apartment over the weekend so if something happened they would all be together for validation.

"I've got to grab a few things downstairs," Greg said. "I'll be right back."

Greg entered his apartment and immediately felt goose bumps run down his neck and arms. A sweet powdery odor of perfume permeated his apartment; it was distinctly feminine. Greg backed up against his living room wall and looked around but could see nothing. He felt a presence, there was no denying it. *Nope,* he said to himself, *not staying here.* It all happened so fast he surprised himself. He packed a bag and bolted to his car, saying nothing to his comrades upstairs. He pointed his car in the direction of his parent's and sped through the neighborhood. He had to leave. He had no choice. At least, that is what he told himself when the thoughts of acting like a coward lept forward. His throat felt tight and he was nocuous. All he knew was that he could not say in the apartment and nobody could tell him differently.

Karen stood in her kitchen, with the phone frozen in her hand. Tina was on the other end telling Tina everything that had happened the last three weeks and what they had just discovered today. Tina couldn't believe what she was hearing and was not sure how to guide Tina.

"I'm not sure what you want me to do, Tina," Karen said. "I don't think it's a good idea for you to come to the house right now until we get this figured out. If you were followed by something, I don't want it to come here. I'm sorry if that sounds selfish but it's how I feel right now. I have to protect Brandi and Billy."

Tina internally reacted, she felt hurt and offended for a moment but also understood. If this spirit latched onto someone else right now she wouldn't want to have it back either! Trying to keep herself under some emotional control, Tina attempted to calmly ask what she should do but what came out of her mouth was a loud screech, "What can I do Karen? You can't leave me out to dry, something happened the night I had dinner with you. It started happening on my way home! I don't know what to do."

Karen felt horrible. She could hear Tina begin to cry on the other end of the line. Karen knew this was absolutely the last thing Tina needed to be dealing with. It was the last thing anyone should have to deal with. She knew it was her fault Tina was being haunted.

"Try to stay calm Tina. I'll call Lizzy and see if she has any ideas. We did a house blessing here yesterday, but I don't know if it helped."

"Why did you do a house blessing?" Tina asked confused.

Karen didn't want to go into it under the circumstances. It seemed clear to her that whatever it was had hitched a ride with Tina. *No wonder things have been quiet here for the last three weeks,* Karen thought.

Swallowing her pride Karen decided to relay the whole story to Tina. "Tina, I'm sorry but she may have hitched a ride to your house. Since you may have already taken her, it appears that our house blessing may have been for nothing. Well, not for nothing, the house is now blessed but we had hoped that we helped lead her into the light and apparently that didn't happen."

Tina felt relieved even though she was thinking that maybe she should be mad. Maybe she felt better knowing Karen didn't think she was crazy. Getting some validation from Karen had instantly helped her feel stronger.

"I don't know what to do, Karen," Tina said, "I feel helpless."

"Let me see if I can reach Lizzy. Maybe we can do a blessing at your apartment. In the meantime, calm down. I'm glad you are with Anna and Greg. I will get ahold of Lizzy and get back to you." Karen hung up and immediately began texting Lizzy.

Lizzy had to admit she was proud of her first foray into house cleansing. Karen had not had any activity since it was done and she was convinced it worked as it should. Lizzy looked forward to the weekend and was so glad it was Friday. She shuffled papers around on her desk trying to find something to do, when she was interrupted by a text message from Karen; "911 Spirit Alert! Call me ASAP!"

"Oh no," Lizzy sighed. *What does this mean?* She gingerly picked up her phone and called Karen. The moment Karen answered Lizzy started in, "What happened? Why the alert? Are you and the kids alright? Have you had more activity?"

"No," said Karen, "that's just the point. Even before we blessed the house I haven't had one iota of activity or weird feelings, nothing! Hold on to your hat though because you won't believe what Tina just told me."

"What? What? Tell me!" Lizzy cried into the phone.

" Tina has been plagued with issues since leaving my house three weeks ago when she stopped in for dinner. In fact the other residents at her triplex are experiencing something and there have never been any issues up to this point."

Lizzy was dumbfounded. "So, what are you saying? You think she hitched a ride with Tina to college?" Lizzy said sarcastically.

"Actually yes, that is exactly what I think! Lizzy, can that happen? Can a spirit jump from one place or person to the next?" Karen was intrigued but also scared.

"I'm not the freaking wizard of Oz you know!" Lizzy said loudly. All she could think was she had failed. She hadn't pointed any spirit towards the light. Apparently there was nothing in Karen's home by the time they did the blessing.

"I don't know if it's possible or not. It seems it might be. I can do more research I guess."

"Look Lizzy, I don't know if we have time for that. We have to help Tina. She picked it up at my house. This is the last thing Tina needs in her life! I feel so terrible and helpless. I feel like it's my fault."

"Ok, ok, calm down! We can head up there tomorrow morning and do a blessing on the apartment if you want to. Will the other tenants cooperate? I mean we need to go through the whole place to be sure." Lizzy felt her anxiety creeping in, a dark emptiness she got when she felt she had failed at something. She felt guilty and out of her realm of knowledge.

What was I thinking when I thought I could just bless a house and make it all better? I'm such and idiot, and now I'm getting in deeper into this and I have no idea what the hell I am doing! Lizzy put her head in her hand feeling completely defeated.

"I obviously don't really know what I'm doing. I don't know if I can help them or not. I'll call you when I get off work and we'll make a plan," Lizzy said softly.

"Lizzy, don't get down on yourself. I can hear it in your voice. There was no way for us to know this spirit moved on. I still needed the house blessed. I do feel more protected now and you helped set that up. I know this is all new to you, but you are an Ordained Minister and wasn't this kind of thing one of the reasons you went through Ordination? You wanted to help people spiritually?"

Lizzy wasn't sure anymore about anything. Her eclectic, Metaphysical/Christian belief system seemed sometimes created more questions than answers. Lizzy couldn't get comfortable in her chair and couldn't concentrate on her work. Breathing deeply, she said a little prayer for direction. She felt totally lost.

Like a sprinter waiting for the starting gun to fire, at five minutes to five, Lizzy was gathered up and ready to go. She had been distracted all afternoon. The feelings of insecurity hung inside her like an old dress.

After a long disjointed day, Lizzy was relieved to arrive home. She kicked off her shoes and headed straight for her bag. She made sure everything she needed for the blessing was there. *My little bag of tricks,* she thought, as she patted the bag feeling she had done all she could for now when she had an idea. She grabbed the phone and called Karen, "Hello, I have an idea."

"Hello, tell me," said Karen.

"I think we need a Medium to go with us tomorrow. I just feel like my radar is completely off. I was so proud of myself after we did your house blessing. When I realized the spirit wasn't even there anymore and I hadn't picked up on that, I felt, well, like a failure. I would just like to have some additional confirmation or even better some real information from the spirit if we can get it. I don't think I'm that person. I don't see dead people. That has never been my gift even though I wished it were. I hear them once in awhile but I'm just not consistent."

"You're not a failure Lizzy. You're so damn hard on yourself. You can't be an expert at everything. I've heard you lament this before. You don't see dead people, so what."

"I guess. My idea is to call my friend Janet and see if she can join us. I know it's short notice but I wanted to check with you before I asked her." Lizzy tapped her fingers on the table hoping her idea would go off well.

"It's fine with me. You certainly don't need my permission Lizzy. We are just doing our best to deal with a strange situation. I think we all feel out of sorts at this point. The more the merrier I say!"

"I'll call Janet. I'll pick you up at 8:00 am tomorrow morning and we'll drive to Tina's. If Janet can go, she'll be with me."

"Sounds good Lizzy. I'll call Tina and see you in the morning."

Lizzy felt a little funny calling Janet and blurting this idea out but she just had a feeling Janet could help them. Janet had always known she had some unique gifts. Ever since she was a little girl, she would hear voices, see images and would get goose bumps down her arms when she had a premonition or psychic impression. She had told Lizzy of a couple experiences she felt she had with the spirit world. She believed she had communicated with a friend's husband who had passed suddenly. She also had encountered what she believed to be a young apparition of a boy in her friend's yard.

"You know I'm not a professional or anything, right?" said Janet.

"Who's professional here?" Lizzy spouted. "We need to help Tina and I feel that you might pick up on some information that could help us. I feel like my radar is off and you seem to have a natural talent for this." Lizzy paced the floor in excitement as she talked to Janet and began to see her mish mash of a plan taking some shape.

CHAPTER 9

When Greg smelled the perfume in his apartment and felt weird like someone was watching him his first and only reaction was to bolt. It's funny how fast a person can move when they are scared. Greg packed a bag for the weekend and was in the seat of his car in 4 minutes flat. He was fifteen minutes from his parent's house. He took a deep breath, *Calm down dude! You don't even believe in ghosts!* His parents, Tom and Deanna Hoskins, lived a few miles out of town. Greg called his Mother. "Mom? It's me, your son."

"I know who you are Greg, you goof ball!" Deanna said laughing out loud. "If my caller ID didn't clue me in, uhm let's see, my keen intuition as your mother probably recognized your voice!"

"I'm coming home for the weekend." He said flatly.

Deanna could hear in his voice that he was stressed about something. "Ok, Son, we'd love to have you. Is everything all right?"

"Yes. Everything is fine, just fine. My neighbors have just been a little noisy this last few weeks and I'm tired and thought I might sleep better there."

"Oh, so the girls are partying harder than the boy these days, huh?" Deanna said with a little sarcasm.

"I guess," Greg said quietly.

"Are you on your way now?" Deanna asked.

"Yes, is that ok?" Greg said feeling an odd sense of panic.

"Of course it's OK! We're just getting ready to run out to Rudy's for dinner. If you want to join us then meet us there, we should be there in about 15 minutes."

"Will do, Mom." Greg hung up the phone and pressed down hard on the accelerator. He wanted to get as much distance between him and his apartment as he could. His mind took off like a horse out of the gate. *What was that perfume I smelled? If there really was a spirit in in the building, can we get rid of it somehow? Should I move?"* The questions flooding his head simultaneously.

"Shake it off man!" Greg said out loud. He reached over and cranked up the radio. Rudy's Café was just a few miles away and he could relax with his family. He felt odd and a little light headed but his stomach had calmed down. He was actually surprised by his reaction to the whole incident at the apartment. *Fear is a funny animal,* he thought. When he believed the girls were being loud and inconsiderate he was simply annoyed. When he realized they weren't the culprits, a cascade of feelings had taken over. He didn't think he even believed in spirits or that kind of stuff, but he knew in his gut that those girls were not lying to him. He wasn't the one making the noises and he believed them when they told him they weren't doing it either. He pushed down any guilty feelings about leaving the girls there by themselves. All he knew is he absolutely had to get out of there. He pulled into Rudy's Café on old Hwy 45. His parents would be there shortly and maybe he would begin to feel normal again.

After dinner, Greg followed his parents back to the house. He had hardly spoken through dinner, which was a complete deviation from his normal jovial, social self. Tom and Deanna talked about it briefly on their way home and concluded that he must be exhausted from his neighbor's partying.

The three of them walked into their living room and were hit immediately with a strong aroma. The blood drained from Greg's face immediately. The only other person in the room that seemed as shocked and alarmed as Greg, strangely, was his father.

"Why does our house smell like Love's Baby Soft?" Deanna blurted out.

Tom couldn't move. He stood frozen in his living room unable to take another breath. He reached over and put his hand on the back of his La-Z-Boy to steady himself. Deanna was smiling when she turned around until she saw her husband and son's faces. "What is it you two? You're white as ghosts!"

Greg and Tom looked at each other in horror but didn't respond. "Tom, Greg, what is the matter with you two?" Her brows furrowed over her bright blue eyes. Tom and Greg simultaneously said "Nothing!"

Deanna flipped the lock on the living room window and opened it as wide as it would go. "Now, we'll get a little fresh air in here!" She walked to the kitchen and put their leftovers into the refrigerator.

Tom held his breath for another moment and then moved slowly into his chair.

"I'm going to take a shower Dad, and hit the sack. I've had a really long week," said Greg.

Tom just nodded still unable to speak.

Greg took the stairs two at a time and locked the bathroom door behind him. The warm water felt good. Greg took a deep breath and again told himself to calm down and stop letting his imagination get away with him. On the other hand, his Mother recognized the perfume and said it by name. Greg had seen that his father was noticeably shaken. *Did he feel something?* Greg thought. *Something what? It's just some perfume but why was it following me around.* And then it hit him like a ton of bricks, *Oh shit, it has followed me here!*

Deanna came out of the kitchen and felt something weird in the air. "Tom, do you feel that?"

"What?" Tom finally croaked from his chair.

"I don't know exactly," said Deanna, "I just feel kind of creepy. Why would the house smell like Love's Baby Soft when we came home? I haven't smelled that perfume since I was in high school!"

It was all Tom could do to shrug his shoulders. He swallowed hard as the hairs on the back of his neck stood straight up. He couldn't move. Deanna popped a DVD into the player.

"Is Greg coming back down?"

"I think he's showering and going to bed. That's what he said," Tom said quietly.

Deanna leaned back into the sofa and hit play. She loved having Greg home.

Greg sat straight up in bed. Something startled him. He looked at the clock, 3:33 am. *Is that supposed to mean something?* He wondered. And then, there it was, four loud knocks on his bedroom door. His heart was in his throat as he jumped out of bed and then cautiously put his hand on the doorknob and pulled the door open as fast as he could. Across the hall, his father was doing the same thing. They looked at each other dumb founded.

"Dad," asked Greg, "did you just knock on my door?"

Tom once again couldn't speak. His mouth was frozen. All he could do was shake his head. His heart was pounding so hard he thought he might just keel over right there in the doorway, right in front of his son and wife. Greg could see Deanna now poking her head out from underneath Tom's frozen arm.

"Greg, that's not funny!" she said with her stern 'you're in trouble and I'm ready to use your middle name' voice.

"It wasn't me, Mom, I swear!" Greg said. "Dad, should we check the rest of the house out?"

Tom didn't know why he was feeling so strange. He looked at his son, who clearly heard the knocking and had no idea what to say. He actually did not want to check out the rest of the house. He wanted to push his heart back down out of his throat and run screaming from the house. *Better toughen up!* he thought.

"Honey, we're going to do a walk through and be right back," Tom said slowly.

"Why? Do you think someone is in the house?" Deanna asked now beginning to panic. She thought Greg was playing a trick, she hadn't thought for a minute that someone might be in the house.

"Honey, we don't know. We all heard the knocking, so I think it warrants checking out the rest of the house, don't you?" Tom asked loudly.

"Yes, of course!" said Deanna.

"Go inside the room and lock the door," said.

Greg and Tom went room to room turning on the lights and checking the closets. Oddly, this basic ritual seemed to calm Greg. Tom peered into the bathroom and winced as he quickly pulled the shower curtain back, half expecting something to jump out at him. He was immediately relieved when he confirmed the empty space behind the curtain. Greg checked the guest room with the same results. Father and son met each other at the top of the stairs after sweeping their second floor. They gave each other a sideways glance and both laughed nervously. Tom moved down the stairs first with Greg right behind him. As they reached the landing, they both got a huge whiff of Love's Baby Soft perfume. Their eyes widened as they looked at each other again, not knowing what to say.

Tom shook his head. "Why is that smell here?" Greg just shrugged, he had no idea what the smell was or what it meant. All he knew is that whatever it was, it had followed him to his parent's house and now they were being harassed! He felt guilty. What had he done? He didn't know if he should tell his Father or not. *What if he just thinks I'm flat out crazy?*

The house was clear and the two men had no explanation for what had happened. Neither son nor father was saying everything he was thinking.

"Ok, the coast seems clear. Let's hit the rack son!" Tom patted Greg on the back at the top of the stairs and headed to his room. He was sure he wasn't going to sleep one second the rest of the night. He figured it would take him a few hours just to get his heart and mind to calm down. Tom slid into bed. Deanna cuddled up next to him and he hugged her close.

"There was nothing there of course," he whispered.

Deanna didn't know what to think, "Let's get some sleep."

CHAPTER 10

Tina felt the warmth of the sun on her face as she woke up Saturday morning on Anna's couch. She was up, for the first time in three weeks, having had a good night of uninterrupted sleep. Anna had quietly crept out into the kitchen and started some coffee.

"Good morning sunshine," Tina chirped.

"Morning," responded Anna.

"What do you think about last night?" said Tina wondering if Anna had a good night's sleep as well.

"You mean the distinct sound of SILENCE?" Anna said as she motioned to the coffee pot.

"Sure," said Tina. "I like it black. And yes, for the first time in three weeks I had glorious uninterrupted sleep!"

"Well maybe whatever it is, has to take a rest once in a while," Anna said, not actually believing what she was saying.

"I need to text Greg and tell him he has to come back for this house blessing, or cleansing, or whatever it is Karen and her friends are going to do," Tina said sipping her coffee as she reached for her phone.

"Do you think he'll come back?" Anna asked as she plopped down in the chair across from Tina.

"I don't know. I can't believe he left in the first place. Especially since we had just talked about staying together. I thought I would feel a little safer with him here. Clearly we did fine on our own," said Tina with pride.

Anna laughed, "Oh yeah, Greg, the great protector! He was gone so fast, I couldn't believe it! He didn't even have the balls to tell us he was leaving. Now here we are, the women, holding down the fort!"

"Don't be too hard on him," said Tina. "He's a good guy. He obviously just got spooked."

Tina was concerned because Karen said to have the three residents there Saturday so the whole house could be blessed. If Greg didn't come back, his apartment would not be included and that would mean the blessing would be a waste of time. *How could he just leave us and not even say anything at all when he left!* Tina pondered the "Greg Issue" and began texting him.

"Greg my friend is coming to do a blessing on the triplex but we need you here. Will you please come back? They will be here around 11:00 am."

Lizzy couldn't believe the beautiful day that greeted her. The sky was particularly clear and blue. Lizzy picked up Karen and sprinkled a little holy water on her as she got in the car. "Hey! What are you doing?" Karen said surprised.

"It's a little holy water. It's supposed to enhance our protection."

"Maybe give a girl some warning!" Karen dropped into the seat and stuck her coffee into the cup holder.

"I have to pick up Janet; she agreed to do this with us this morning. Isn't that great!" beamed Lizzy.

"It is great. Are you sure, you have everything you need for the ceremony?"

"Yup," Lizzy steered the car toward Janet's house.

Lizzy introduced Janet as she got into the car and gave her a good splash of holy water as well.

"Oh my! I guess that is kind of refreshing," Janet laughed.

"In all seriousness," Lizzy lowered her voice and pulled out some anointing oil from her bag. "We need to say a prayer of protection anytime we are doing this kind of work. We need to be mindful and reverent. I don't think God will care that I had a little fun getting the holy water on you but this is important."

Dipping her finger into the anointing oil, Lizzy placed a cross on each of their foreheads and prayed for them to be surrounded in holy light and protection.

"It's important that we always remember to do this before we go into any homes or deal with anyone who has been haunted. It's a good practice to just do it daily, don't you think?" Lizzy said and both Karen and Janet agreed.

The hour trip went by quickly as the women discussed the paranormal activities. "It's all a little surreal," Karen said shaking her head.

Janet fiddled with her glasses. "I'm a little nervous. I've never tried to use my gifts in this way. I don't know if I'll be helpful or pick up anything. I hope I don't let you down."

"You can't let us down, Janet," Karen patted her on the shoulder.

"Janet," Lizzy said looking at her in the rear view mirror, "you are one of the most giving people I know. I'm not worried. You will feel what you feel. If you don't pick up on anything, don't worry about it. What is supposed to happen will happen. We all want to help. I think that is the most important intention. I believe our intent is the most important thing we put out there and our intent is to be of service and help bring in light where there may be darkness. Together we can only be stronger."

CHAPTER 11

The triplex felt impending to Lizzy as they pulled into the driveway. Would it be if she didn't think it was haunted? Maybe not, maybe she would think it was beautiful. The tri-colored Victorian house was over 4000 square feet and painted maroon with golden yellow trim with grey blue shutters. Anna's upstairs apartment benefited from the rounded cornices. The eves on the second floor looked like eyebrows over the upper story windows. Were they ominously looking down upon them or innocently projecting beautiful Victorian curves? She couldn't be sure.

Tina and Anna stepped out onto the porch as Karen, Lizzy and Janet began collecting their bags with items to bless the home.

Tina hugged Karen, "Thank you so much for coming."

"Of course," said Karen as she hugged Tina. The entourage climbed up the steps on to the porch and shuffled into the house. Anna opened the door and introduced herself, "Hi, I'm Anna; I live in the apartment upstairs. Tina has talked nonstop about all of you and I'm really happy to see you."

"We're happy to be here, Anna. Let's take a look inside," said Lizzy, "and see if Janet can pick up on anything. Then we will begin the blessing."

They all stood in the foyer for a few moments trying to get a feel for the place. Janet began to breathe deeply to calm herself. She said an internal prayer and blessing. She asked to be open to what she needed to connect with, that which would help the most. "Something is missing," Janet said, feeling a little confused.

"What do you mean?" asked Lizzy quietly.

"I'm not sure," said Janet. Janet turned and looked at Tina and Anna, "There is a piece of this that's missing."

Like deer in the headlights, Anna and Tina stared back at Janet, not knowing what she meant or how to answer. Janet said it again, "There is a piece of the puzzle missing. That is what I'm picking up. What is missing?"

Then it occurred to Anna that maybe it wasn't something but someone. "Greg!" she blurted out.

"Oh yea," said Tina. She pointed to Greg's apartment, "He lives there but he went to his parents last night after we all talked about what we were experiencing."

Janet shook her head, "Lizzy, it's not here. I think it's with Greg."

"What?" Lizzy gasped. "What do you mean? Are you sure?"

Janet walked to Greg's door and placed the palm of her hand on it. "I'm pretty sure it is with him. Was there any activity last night after he left?"

They looked at each other, amazed, and both began shaking their heads.

"In fact," said Anna, "we both commented this morning on how we had finally gotten a full night's sleep."

"What does this mean?" asked Karen. "This spirit suddenly has begun hopping from person to person? What the hell?"

Lizzy wasn't sure what to think.

Janet nodded. "I feel she left with Greg."

Lizzy's head began to spin. *What now? How will we be able to help anyone if we can't find the spirit?*

"Janet, do you get anything else?" asked Karen.

"I don't feel a presence of any sort but I do feel Greg was very scared when he left. He in fight or flight and his choice was flight."

"I think from the beginning he was the most freaked out of the three of us," said Anna.

"Yes, once we all figured out none of us were making the noises and knocking on the walls, he got very uptight," said Tina. "The plan was that we were all going to stay with each other until you could get up here to do the blessing. He left right after we met with Anna and actually never told us he was leaving."

"When was that?" asked Lizzy feeling frustrated.

"Last night," replied Anna.

"We should still do the blessing, shouldn't we Lizzy? I mean it would help keep her from coming back, wouldn't it?" asked Karen.

"I agree," said Lizzy. "We've come all the way here and it certainly won't hurt to do the blessing. I don't know if it will keep her out when Greg comes back though. If it doesn't, you girls can do the blessing again yourselves."

Janet began moving toward Tina's apartment door and put her hand on it. "Have either of you talked to Greg since he left?"

"No, we texted him last night and this morning about you all coming today but he never responded," said Tina.

"Let's do the blessing," said Janet. "I think it will accomplish what you hope, here. I have a funny feeling about Greg. It would be better if he joined us."

CHAPTER 12

Greg jolted awake, he heard his mother yelling.

"Tom! Tom! Tom, come here!" Once again, Tom and Greg were both at their bedroom doors looking at each other alarmed. Deanna was standing in the hallway in front of the bathroom pointing at the doorway.

"Mom what is it?" Greg said loudly as he rushed to his mother's side.

"Did one of you do that?" she shrieked. She knew the answer already, but had to make sure.

Greg crept through the bathroom door. His mother's makeup was all over the floor and in the tub. Someone or something had written 'JOSHNOW' on the mirror with one of his mother's red lipsticks. He backed out of the bathroom into the hall.

Tom went through the same maneuver, and when he saw the mirror, he caught his breath.

"What the hell is going on?" croaked Deanna. "Last night, now this?"

Greg knew exactly what was going on. Whatever had been at his apartment was now in his parent's house! It was entirely his fault!

Tom still couldn't move. He stood transfixed in front of the mirror his mouth agape. Then, like a soft breeze, the smell of

Loves Baby Soft filled the bathroom and then whole upstairs. When the scent hit Tom's olfactory center, his knees buckled and he grabbed the doorframe to steady himself.

"Come out of there Tom!" Deana yelled her nerves now raw. When the aroma of Loves Baby Soft filled the upstairs, the hair on the back of her neck stood up and Goosebumps ran up her arms. "I don't know what the hell is going on here but we need to get out of here right now!" said Deanna.

Tom quickly backed out of the bathroom and made it to his bedroom in a daze.

"Greg, get your clothes on we're going to breakfast," Deanna yelled from the bedroom.

"You don't need to twist my arm, let's go!" He turned on his heel and got dressed quickly.

Deanna grabbed Tom's jeans and threw them to him. "Get dressed we're getting out of here." Deanna pulled on a ball cap without combing her hair. There was no way she was going into that bathroom. They moved quickly and dashed to the car in less than five minutes. No one said a word all the way to Rudy's Diner.

Tom broke into a cold sweat driving to Rudy's. *How does that happen?* He thought, *Cold sweat? It's not right. Cold and sweat shouldn't happen at the same time. Now I'm rambling in my own head. Calm down, calm, Tom.*

Tom couldn't escape his guilt. He had been feeling it, full force, since the night before when he smelled the perfume for the first time. He had managed to bury his guilt and shame for many years but every now and then, something would trigger his memories. Love's Baby Soft wafting through his home broke the final straw. It was his fault and he knew it.

I was a coward and now it is being forced into the open, he thought. He would have to talk to Deanna, confess his sins and hope that she would forgive him. Right now, he just wanted to run. He hadn't felt this awful in 25 years. *Isn't that amazing, there is low, and then there is lower than low.* Tom wiped the beads of sweat from his brow as he pulled into Rudy's Café. *Grab some coffee and get your shit together, after breakfast, talk to Deanna.*

Greg's emotions were running high, he actually felt like crying.   He could hear his heart pounding in his ears but did not understand what was happening. What he did know is that he brought something home and he was very sorry. How could he tell his parents? Would they be angry for his irresponsibility?

Rudy's was in full rush when they walked into the dining area. The smell of bacon broke the spell for a moment.

Helen, their favorite server, motioned them in as she cleared off a booth in the back corner.

"Hello folks!" Helen said cheerfully. "Sit right on down and I'll be with you in a minute. I'm gonna assume you want coffee." They all nodded and slid into the booth.

"Dad? I need to tell you and Mom about something but you might want to put me in a straight jacket."

"Greg, I think after the last 12 hours we all could use a nice, quiet, padded room. We're listening son, shoot."

Greg gulped his words back as Helen slid up to the table and plunked down three coffees and some menus.

"I'll be back for your order. Deanna, how you doing this morning? You look a fright!" laughed Helen.

Deanna frowned, "Thanks Helen, it's been a rough night."

"Oh sweetie, with a family like this it can't be that bad!" She fluttered off into the kitchen.

Deanna felt weird. "What did you want to tell us Greg?" she asked.

"I don't know where to start. A few weeks ago, I started hearing a lot of noise at night. I thought it was the girls in the triplex. We've all lived there about a year I guess, and have all gotten along fine. Anna pretty much keeps to herself and Tina is nice. Anyway, about three weeks ago I began hearing what I thought was furniture being moved around their apartments.

76

Sometimes it would be in Tina's apartment and then sometimes it was in Anna's. It would go on sometimes until past 3 o'clock in the morning. Then there was the knocking. I could hear someone knocking on their doors constantly. Sometimes I would hear knocking on the wall that separated our apartments. I was getting pretty frustrated. So finally, yesterday, I went to Tina's to ask her to please 'knock it off!' I've had three hours of sleep a night for the last three weeks…" Greg paused to get a feel for whether his parents were going to tease him or believe him.

Deanna and Tom were listening intently. "Go on," Deanna pushed.

Greg took a deep breath and continued, "Last night I went over to Tina's to ask her to please stop all the noise." Greg looked down at his hands. He realized he had been wringing them as he spoke. He shook his head and sighed.

Just then, Helen swooped in to take their order. Helen, a tall woman in her mid-fifties ran around the restaurant like a teenager. She had been at Rudy's for as long as Greg could remember. She had always been very upbeat and loud!

"Lay it on me guys, what'll ya have?"

Greg and his parents placed their order quickly and Helen hurried off to hang the ticket.

"Go on Greg," Tom urged.

"Well, Tina said she wasn't doing it. She said she had heard the same thing coming from my apartment and Anna's as well. While we were talking we heard knocking in my apartment. There was no one in my apartment. When we went to my apartment to investigate, the knocking came from her apartment. We decided to talk to Anna and she said she had heard the same things. Tina said she had a friend she thought could help and would call her. In the meantime, we were going to stay at Anna's, so we had witnesses to our experiences if anything else happened. We were all a little freaked out at this point. I went downstairs to get some stuff for the night but when I walked into my apartment it smelled like that perfume…what you said Mom, that Loves Baby Soft. Then…I just got the creepiest feeling as if someone was watching me and I

77

bolted. I came home and I'm so sorry because I think it came with me! This BS last night is my fault!" Greg said progressively getting more wound up.

"Calm down Greg," Tom said as he grabbed his son's shoulder and shook him gently.

"It's not your fault."

"Dad, what does 'JO SHNOW' mean? Why was that on the mirror?"

Tom was sure the words were JOSH NOW, not JO SHNOW. He couldn't get into that right now. He needed to talk to Deanna first.

"We'll figure it out son, don't worry."

"I am worried!" Deanna said as she took a shaky sip of coffee. "I want to know what the hell is going on. Why or how would something come home with Greg? Have you ever heard of that?"

Tom shook his head.

Greg shrugged and said, "I don't know but I think it HAS happened."

Tom felt uneasy. He knew it wasn't Greg's fault but he didn't know how to approach it. He didn't understand how Greg got connected to the situation in the first place.

The family smiled politely as Helen plunked the breakfast plates on the table and whizzed away again.

"Let's relax here and eat our breakfast. When we get back home your Mother and I will figure this out."

"We will?" Deanna asked. She was surprised at Tom's confidence. She had no idea how to address this and as far as going home she wasn't very excited about that prospect.

CHAPTER 13

As the Hoskins family neared the front door of their home, their steps in unison, slowed, as they got closer. Tom slid the key in the door and gingerly pushed it open. He couldn't believe what he saw. He pushed Deanna back and said, "Hold on a minute."

"What?" said Deanna intensely.

Tom unconsciously began clenching his jaw. Something was not right in the house. He could hear water running and he could see pictures on the living room floor.

"Shit!" he exclaimed and shot through the door toward the sound of the running water. He reached the kitchen in what seemed like just a few steps and turned the water off. It had not overflowed anywhere, thank goodness!

Deanna gasped as she came through the front door. She stopped cold three steps into her living room. Glancing around in horror, she could see that their cherished wedding photos had been thrown into a pile in the middle of the floor. She did not know whether to get angry or cry. A combination of confused emotions swirled insider her. Tom rounded the corner on his way to the downstairs bathroom to turn the water off.

"Deanna, will you go upstairs and see if the water is on in the bathroom?"

"Nope, I'm not going anywhere without you, nor am I going up there by myself," she said emphatically. Tom knew the look she was giving him was a mixture of fear and stubbornness and she could be stubborn!

"I'll go," said Greg. He didn't want to go upstairs by himself either but he wasn't going to let on. He took the stairs three at a time. In what seemed like one movement, he turned the water off in the sink and tub and was back at the railing making his way down the stairs. Cleaning the red lipstick on the mirror with 'JOSHNOW' written on it would have to wait.

The three stood in the living room looking dazed and confused.

"What now?" asked Deanna.

"I probably should have said something earlier, but the girls from my triplex texted me last night saying they had some people coming to do a blessing on the apartments to see if they could get rid of the spirit. They texted me again while we were at breakfast. They want me there so they can go through the whole place."

"Under the circumstances, Greg, I think you should call them and let them know what is going on," Tom said, even though he was having a hard time believing it himself.

Greg dialed Tina and stepped onto the front porch to talk. The house did not feel very inviting.

"Can they come here and help us?" asked Deanna. She began picking up the pictures off the floor and started hanging them back in place. "This is ridiculous! I'm so freaked out!"

"I know," said Tom. Just then, he felt someone or something softly touch his cheek.

Deanna caught Tom out of the corner of her eye. She saw the blood drain from his face.

"What's wrong?"

Tom shook his head back and forth, as he turned to go out to the back patio. "I need a minute to deal." He walked straight to a patio chair at the corner of the deck and sank down with a long sigh. He pulled his wallet from his back pocket. Slowly he removed a yellowed and frayed newspaper clipping from a little secret pocket in his wallet. As he unfolded it, he felt the weight of 20 years of guilt settle on his shoulders. The obituary was relatively long considering she was only 16. There she was, Sunday Stewart, all of 16, dead of an overdose.

"I'm sorry Sunny, I am so sorry!" he whispered.

Deanna worked alone in the living room hanging her wedding pictures back into place. Suddenly, the room filled with the smell of Loves Baby Soft perfume. All the hair on her arms stood straight up creating goose bumps at every follicle. One of the wedding pictures sitting on the mantle propelled itself across the room almost hitting her in the head and landed on the floor.

"That is it!" she shouted into the room and ran out the back door. "It's in there again," Deanna yelled to Tom. "The perfume is back and a wedding picture took a flying leap off the mantle all by itself and almost hit me in the head! What are we going to do?"

Tom wrapped his arms around his wife. He loved her so much, how would he be able to tell her what he'd done?

"Let's see what Greg's friends have to say," Tom said as he folded up the newspaper clipping back into his wallet.

Tina yelled out, " It's Greg, he's finally calling."

Just in time, Lizzy thought since they were just about done with the first two apartments. She felt it was important for them to bless the whole house as well pray for protection.

Anna moved to Tina's side so she could listen as Tina talked to Greg. There were a lot of 'uh huhs' and 'what's going ons?' Tina's face was somber as she hung up with Greg.

"He's on his way. You won't believe what he just told me. Now Greg's parent's house is haunted! Everything that was going on here has been going on there since Greg arrived home. His parents are beside themselves and Greg is feeling so guilty he doesn't know what to say or do. He feels he took it over there."

"He did," said Lizzy, "but, he can't blame himself. I had never heard of a ghost hitchhiking around before this. I did do a little research last night and I guess it isn't all that uncommon. I am glad he will be here to finish this blessing."

"Greg wants to know if you would go to his parent's house and maybe help them there?" Tina asked Karen.

"Lizzy, we can do that can't we?" Karen asked.

"Of course! We're here, we might as well finish this thing out," said Lizzy.

Tom and Deanna sat on the back porch for a few minutes and then decided to brave the house. They approached the living room and found all their wedding pictures were in a pile on the floor again.

"Oh come on!" exclaimed Deanna in frustration. "I just hung all this back up!"

"I'll help you," Tom said picking up one of the pictures and setting it on the mantle. He remembered his wedding day like it was yesterday. He smiled despite the odd circumstances going on in his home.

"This was a great day, Deanna."

"Yes, it was," she smiled back. They moved toward each other and embraced.

"It's going to be ok," said Tom. "I do love you. You know that, right?" he asked.

Deanna pushed back from his chest, looked up into his worried eyes and nodded. Deanna noticed he was acting a little strange. The whole morning was strange, of course, but she was just picking up on something else.

Tom received a text from Greg letting him know they would be coming back to the house to do a blessing.

"Let's just wait to see what Greg has to say after they bless the apartment house. We should get ready to meet these people who are helping out. Greg says they will come here next." Tom moved toward the couch. The picture he just set on the mantle fell to the floor, again. Tom dropped down on the couch and motioned for Deanna to come sit next to him.

"Just leave them on the floor for now. I have a feeling this is going to keep happening until we are able to address the real issue."

"What the heck would that be?" asked Deanna.

"I guess we'll have to wait and see what these 'ghost busters' have to say," he said. He hoped the issue could be figured out without him having to make a big confession. He knew in his heart that some things he had tried to bury were working their way into the light of day. If he could keep them buried, he would.

CHAPTER 14

Greg pulled into his parking spot at the triplex. Tina flew out the front door and wrapped her arms around him, giving him a big unexpected hug.

"Are you ok?" she asked.

"I don't know," Greg shot back. "I didn't get any sleep again last night. You can't believe everything that went on at my parent's house. When I realized what had happened, that I had taken it there, I felt so bad!"

"I know," said Tina. "I felt the same way when I realized I was the one who brought it here. I'm so sorry!"

"It's not your fault, obviously this thing, whatever it is, just latches on to people and takes a ride. I'm so creeped out I don't know if I'm coming or going!" Greg said.

"We're almost done blessing the house. Karen is like my second mother. Lizzy, her friend, is a Minister and Janet is a psychic." Tina was talking a hundred miles an hour now, "Janet, the psychic, said immediately something was missing and we didn't know what she meant and then we realized it was you!"

"Ok, ok, slow down there, you're gonna hyperventilate!" Greg said patting Tina on the shoulder.

Tina took a slow deep breath as they stepped into the foyer. She hadn't realized she was so wound up. Inside the foyer, the group was waiting for Greg and Tina.

Greg walked through the door and Janet immediately said, "So you're the missing one! I see you dropped your baggage off before you came back here."

"What do you mean?" asked Greg feeling confused.

Janet looked at Lizzy and Karen, "She's not with him."

"Greg," said Lizzy, "may we bless your apartment and then talk about your parent's situation?"

"Sure," he said, unlocking his apartment door and pushing his way inside. "Make yourself at home." He motioned them all to go in. They stepped into his kitchen. There was no perfume smell and he felt nothing. He hoped that was a good sign. The entourage walked single file through each room with the blessings and prayers of protection, and then finished up in the foyer.

Lizzy blessed the foyer and they all moved onto the porch where Lizzy sprinkled salt in front of the main doors. They prayed for a barrier of protection against anything negative.

"Greg, why did you leave last night?" asked Lizzy.

"I just completely lost my cool. I came downstairs after talking to the girls and I got this overwhelming whiff of perfume. My mother says its Loves Baby Soft. It was at their house last night when we came home from dinner. My Mom knew the name of the perfume. I smelled it and felt like someone was standing right next to me in my apartment and I just bolted!" Greg looked down at his feet. "I feel ashamed that I left the girls here alone. I wasn't thinking. I just knew I couldn't stay here one more minute."

Greg began relating the events of the past 24 hours. They all listened, riveted by his story.

"Ok," said Lizzy, "we are willing to help, but just so you know, we are amateurs. We will do what we can but I can't guarantee anything. "

85

"Greg," asked Janet, "may I touch your hand?"

"Sure."

Janet placed her hand on Greg's and took slow breaths. "We need to go to your parent's house. She is there."

"How do we know it's a 'she'?" asked Greg.

"We've all felt it. That has been the impression we've all had so far," said Anna.

"Admittedly, I felt the same thing," said Greg. "Let's get this show on the road then. You can follow me to my parent's house."

Tina and Anna jumped in Greg's car. The women gathered up their 'blessing bags' and hopped into Lizzy's car and were off to the next adventure.

"Oh, wow," commented Janet. "I just had the most overwhelming feeling of sadness. Lizzy, I'm feeling some trepidation about this meeting. I feel so sad and I'm not sure what to expect."

"None of us knows what to expect at this point Janet," said Lizzy. She wondered to herself, *What have I gotten us into?*

Karen had not said much during the blessing. Although she wanted to help Tina, she secretly wished she could bow out. "This is a lot of drama. I wish we could go home."

Janet leaned in from the front seat, "The drama isn't over yet, sorry. I feel there is more to come when we get to Greg's parent's house. There is something more, something being hidden. I just feel it."

"I feel pretty convinced the spirit is Sunday Stewart. It all fits. Mary told me it was a sad situation. Sunday's brother found her when he got home from school. The family left the house and moved back east shortly after Sunday's death. It tore the family up, which is understandable." Lizzy said. She couldn't imagine finding her sibling dead nor could she imagine how a parent lived through such a terrible loss.

"I feel like it was an accident," said Janet.

"What do you mean?" asked Karen. "I thought she left a note. I thought she killed herself?"

"She didn't mean to die. She didn't think she would actually die," Janet responded.

"Let's see what you pick up when we get there. All of us need to be on 'psychic alert'," said Lizzy.

Karen squirmed in her seat. "My gut hurts, is that alert enough for you? Let's not do this."

Lizzy felt nervous as well but knew they couldn't turn back now, "We HAVE to finish this. I really feel we have to help them, especially since it kind of originated at your house."

"I know. I know," Karen said totally exasperated. "I just don't know how this could be happening to me, us…it's surreal. For the record, it did not originate at my house. It originated from Justin Blake's house." She did not want to participate further. She wanted out of this drama and the sooner the better.

"Looks like we're here," Lizzy said as they slowed to a stop behind Greg.

Greg's parent's house was a cozy-looking Craftsman built in the mid 40's. It was painted a brownish grey with grey-blue trim. It had a cottage feel. The front yard was adorned with a quaint flower garden. Greg led the way as Tina and Anna followed close behind. Lizzy, Karen and Janet grabbed their bags and walked toward the house. Deanna stood in the doorway as the entourage approached.

"Welcome," Deanna said with a half-smile trying to act relaxed. She led everyone into the living room. Right away, Lizzy noticed a thick feeling in the air. Janet reached out and touched her arm as they gathered in the coffered ceiling living room. The home was quite beautiful. In the middle of the floor was a pile of wedding and family pictures.

"Please sit down," Deana motioned to the couch and love seat. I will go get Tom."

The distinct odor of Loves Baby Soft spun through the air. Lizzy, Janet and Karen all looked at each other, eyebrows raised.

"I haven't smelled that since high school!" exclaimed Karen.

"I know," Lizzie said, "I used to wear that!" It was funny how that smell brought back a hundred memories of her own teen years. *Oh, the angst and all the intense feelings*, Lizzy remembered. "I'm glad those days are behind me." Karen and Janet agreed.

"The pictures were like this when we got home from breakfast this morning," Greg pointed out.

Tom and Deanna entered the room. Tom, a tall attractive man in his mid-forties was just beginning to show speckles of grey in his thick dark hair. He had a strong athletic build. Greg was fortunate to inherit much of his father's DNA. Tom, however, did look noticeably drained. Lizzy could feel that his energy was very low. She supposed it stood to reason after having a night of spirit antics keeping them all from sleeping.

"Hello, I'm Tom Hoskins," he thrust his large hand out and enveloped each woman's hand as he gently shook each one. When he got to Janet, she took his hand with both of her hands and held it. She looked deep into his eyes and perceived a secret.

How am I supposed to deal with this? she thought, almost out loud. Janet got a strong sense of a young girl's energy attached to his aura. Tom finally gently pulled his hand away. They all sat down. Everyone introduced themselves one by one.

"Janet is an Intuitive, a Psychic," Lizzy explained. "We want you to know that we're here to help in any way we can, however, we also need you to know we are new at this. This is literally my, well my third 'case'. I must say, my first case was in Karen's house. I was quite proud of myself thinking I had blessed and cleared the house of this spirit. Of course, I realized the blessing I did had no effect on the spirit because this spirit has been attaching herself to people and moving around. I don't believe she has actually been in any of the locations we've blessed so far."

"She's here now!" Janet blurted out loudly. "She is next to Tom." Tom felt self-conscious. He looked around but saw nothing. What he felt, however, was something else.

"So, my point is," continued Lizzy, "we will bless the house but we don't guarantee anything."

"You know more than we do at this point," said Tom, "so I feel comfortable in your hands as long as Deanna is in agreement."

"Of course I'm in agreement," Deanna shot back.

"Let's begin then," said Lizzy. "We have all felt that this spirit is a teenage girl. After doing some research I believe her name is Sunday Stewart. She died in the mid 90's of a suicide."

Tom noticeably squirmed in his chair and seemed to avoid eye contact with Lizzy.

Janet spoke up, "Before we go any further I need to say something to Tom. This is the first time I've utilized my gift in this way. I never know exactly what or how I will receive information. I feel you are very guarded. I am not sure I should proceed with the information I am getting."

Tom looked down at his hands and fiddled with a piece of string he had found on his shirt. "It's all right," Tom said barely audibly, "It's time. Go ahead with what you need to say. It is important that we get this taken care of and that my family doesn't suffer further due to my mistake."

"Your mistake?" asked Deanna. "What is that supposed to mean?"

"I will tell you all everything I know, but let's first have Janet tell us what she has picked up." Tom said. He was felt a bit of relief knowing the truth was finally coming out. *I hope Deanna and Greg don't hate me when everything is on the table. What if this blessing doesn't work and my family is tormented forever because of my cowardly decisions?* He started to to panic as these thoughts raced through his mind.

Janet asked everyone to change seats so she could sit next to Tom on the couch. She gently took his hands and began calming herself. It was like water flowing through a pipe as she began, "This girl, I see her as a petite blond with blue eyes and a broad smile."

Tom nodded.

What is this? Why is he nodding his head? Did he know this girl? Deanna's mind reeled.

Janet continued, "She is telling me it was an accident. She didn't mean to kill herself, although she was very angry and hurt and wanted to get your attention."

Tom's head hung and a tear rolled down his cheek.

Deanna stood up, her blood boiling, "Tom! What is this? You knew this girl?"

Tom looked up at Deanna and quietly said, "Deanna, please sit down. Let Janet finish. I will explain everything I know, I promise."

Deanna couldn't remember the last time she had witnessed her husband crying. He seemed earnest so she sat down to listen.

Janet felt the soft tingle run up her arms. Goose bumps began to appear. She knew what she was feeling was right on, "So, she is telling me that you broke her heart."

Tom nodded, "I was a coward. I am so sorry I didn't tell you in person. I'm sorry. I've been sorry for 20 years."

"She is showing me a picture of a boy finding her, her brother," Janet was quiet. A long minute passed as she processed the information that was coming to her. "Sunday sat for a long time with him after she died. He was devastated and blamed himself for her death. He believes that if he had come home earlier from school he could have saved her."

Sunday was using all the energy she had to project the information to Janet. She began screaming, "Not true! Not true! He could not have saved me." Sunday had to find a way to reach her brother. If this didn't work, she didn't know what she would do.

Janet continued, "She says, 'Not true.' She had been gone for a while before he discovered her. She was very confused. She didn't realize she was dead at first. She knew something had happened but it wasn't clear to her at the time. Then, she says, her family was gone and she didn't know how to find them. She rambled around in the house, angry and confused."

Tom stood up, "What can I do? I'm so sorry!"

"She says you're still kind of an asshole!" Janet didn't usually curse, especially in front of a group. "Sorry, this is what I'm getting," she said. "This is not actually entirely about you Tom, it's more about her brother, her family. She has a message for her brother and she wants you to deliver that message."

"Are you kidding me?" Tom yelled, "Josh hates me!"

"She says that he will listen to you and she doesn't know how to find him."

If Sunday could jump up and down, she would. "You owe me Tom! You owe me!" she yelled into Janet's mind.

Janet picked up Sunday's emotion, "She says, you owe her."

Tom stood motionless. He knew it was true, "Ok."

Deanna spoke up, "Do you want to tell me now what the hell is going on?"

"Yes," said Tom, his eyes cast down at the floor. "I dated her before we met. She was four years younger than I was. I met her the summer before college. She was a nice girl but she was young. And then…. I met you. I didn't know how to tell her."

"Soooo? What? Were you seeing her while we were going out?" asked Deanna feeling her face getting hot.

"No! Yes! Not exactly! I did see her a few times while we were going out but nothing happened and it was before we were committed," Tom put his hand on his head, as he looked deep into Deanna's eyes.

"And…?" Deanna glared at her husband. "You slept with her?"

"How does that matter now? I fell in love with you! Instead of telling her, I just quit calling her," Tom said. He looked down at the floor hoping to avoid his wife's angry eyes. All the pressure from the past and present pushed him to the edge of breaking down.

"So, you did sleep with her?" Deanna asked, thoroughly disgusted.

"It was only once and it was before you and I met." Tom said. He wanted some foothold to defend himself but could find none.

All the women sank back in their seats. They realized they were in the middle of something that they couldn't have predicted. Greg sat silently, not knowing what to say or think as his angry mother stormed at his father.

"So how did she find out?" Deanna yelled back.

"I heard she saw our engagement picture in the paper," Tom said softly.

"Wow!" said Deanna, "You *were* an asshole! I'm sorry Sunday, I had no idea! No wonder she's throwing pictures at my head."

"Doesn't it count that I fell in love with you and married you?" Tom pleaded.

"It does, but Tom," Deanna said hardly knowing how to react to the information, "it's just very, very sad and tragic! I can't imagine what her parents went through."

Janet stood up to meet the couple in the middle of the room. She reached out and clasped their hands.

"Sunday appreciates the sentiment, but she emphasized again that this is not all about you. She needs to reach her brother, her family."

"I need to know," said Tom, "would it have made a difference had I told her in person?"

"You're off the hook Tom. She says she was in love with you and didn't mean to kill herself in the first place. She doesn't know that telling her in person would have changed her reaction. Maybe things would have turned out differently, but the bottom line is, it is too late. She keeps showing me 'Josh Now.' She just wants to get a message to her brother. Will you do it?"

"Josh now?" said Deanna, "that's what she wrote on the mirror, 'JOSH NOW'. "

Tom looked at Deanna, "Are you ok with me finding Josh?"

She nodded, "Of course, help Sunday finish this so she can be in peace."

Lizzy finally piped up, "Do you know how to reach Josh?"

"Not exactly, but I heard he was a counselor here in town. I can find him."

"Does this mean she will be with us until then?" asked Greg, worried about never having a full night's sleep again.

"She says she will quiet down as long as you find her brother so she can talk to him,"

Janet was a little shocked at just how much information was flowing through her. She felt excited and a little frightening at the same time. Was it real or was she just making stuff up? Doubts plagued her. Sunday told her there was something in Tom's wallet.

"What's in your wallet, Tom?" Janet asked.

"What?"

"She says there is something in your wallet that I need to see."

Tom reluctantly reached his wallet and pulled out the weathered newspaper clipping of Sunday's obituary.

"Thanks," said Janet. She knew she couldn't have known about that and it made her feel more confident that the information she was receiving was real. *Trust yourself,* she thought.

Tom dropped back onto the couch and began to cry. His wife and son watched motionless. Greg couldn't ever remember seeing his father cry. Tom wept as over twenty years of guilt and silent grief spilled out. He had always been so sorry for what happened.

Tom spoke out-loud to Sunday, "I did like you Sunny. It was not your fault, there was nothing wrong with you. I just fell in love with someone else and you were so young. I didn't mean for any of this to happen."

Janet patted Tom's hand, "She appreciates that but you still have to talk to her brother."

"I will," said Tom. "I promise to find Josh."

Lizzy handed Tom her card with her cell number, "Call me when you find him and we will set up some kind of meeting."

Tom shook his head, worried, "I'm telling you it might be difficult, this guy can't stand me."

"It will work out. Find Josh and we will find a way to work out the rest," Lizzy said.

They all hugged each other goodbye. Deanna and Tom thanked everyone for their help. Greg, Tina and Anna were grateful and hopeful that their ordeal was over. They all looked forward to uninterrupted sleep.

The three women drove home. Lizzy arrived at Karen's first.

"I'm not coming back," said Karen as she gathered her belongings. "I don't want to be involved in this anymore. I said I would help with the blessing and I did. I hope you understand."

"I do understand, but I can't back out in the middle of this. Are you still in Janet?" asked Lizzy.

"I am," said Janet. She had a deep desire to help others and felt suddenly invigorated with the results her gift had generated that day. "I'm definitely in."

"Thanks for understanding, Lizzy." Karen said.

"If you change your mind…"

"I won't," said Karen. "We'll talk tomorrow."

CHAPTER 15

Josh Stewart, a chiseled specimen of manhood, took a lot of pride in his ability to stay disciplined with his workout routines. Standing 6' 2" with 230 pounds of ripped muscle, unlike his boyish self, he was quite an imposing figure.

He graduated with his Masters in Psychology from Harvard. After his sister died, he had thrown himself into his studies and graduated from high school at the top of his class. He secured a scholarship and between working like a dog and the support from his parents, he graduated from Harvard and became a Licensed Therapist. His passion pushed him to help those who were in pain. His work became his mission to work with teenagers and adults who may be at risk for suicide. He provided a support group for families dealing with the grief and devastation suicide leaves surviving family members.

Who would know better than me? He had often thought as he moved hundreds of clients through their grief process. His sister's death had indeed shaped his path, his life, in more ways than one. Josh met Cynthia his first year attending Harvard. Tall, blonde and smart, he couldn't believe she wanted to be with him. She was his first 'real' girlfriend and his last. Through Junior High and High School Josh sported a short stocky figure. His mother kept telling him he would grow, that the men in their family seemed to bulk up before they grew up. She meant it literally and Josh prayed she was right. His father and uncles were all 6'2" or taller. For years he felt like a troll under the bridge. Awkward and shy through school, Josh had little experience with 'the ladies'. He was the quintessential late bloomer, just as his mother promised, he grew almost ten painful inches between his Junior Year of High School and his first year of college. He remembered he barely recognized himself at times. This added up to a very clueless man where it came to his new effect on women.

Cynthia noticed him right away. A lot of the girls on campus noticed Josh. She knew what she wanted and she got him. They hit if off immediately and he was flattered that this beautiful debutante liked him. At the time, he allowed himself to believe she was the perfect girl for him. They married his sophomore year. Looking back now, he realized that may have been a little premature. After graduation, Josh talked her into moving back to Oregon with him. He set up his practice just an hour from the town where Sunday had died.

Cynthia's family liked Josh well enough but had always felt she married beneath her. She hated Oregon and wanted to move back to Connecticut where her family was quite prolific. The early years of their marriage were filled with school, work, and their combined drive to finish what they had started. Cynthia received her Master's degree in business and had moved quickly up the ladder at a large bank. Everything had moved so fast when they met. Josh liked her and the way she looked, but there were many things between the two that did not connect. She came from money and had certain expectations regarding the style she wanted to live in and persona she desired to portray. Josh had a tough exterior but it simply guarded his sensitive soul. She had pushed to get married quickly and Josh had naively agreed under the pressure. He still liked her and a kind of love had grown between them, but overall the relationship was passionless. After 18 years of marriage, he accepted it as comfortable. They made a nice looking couple with their big smiles and beautiful faces, but as the years wore on it was obvious they had very little in common except they both worked long hours and liked good food. Josh had come to the conclusion years ago that their work schedules may possibly have been the reason their relationship had lasted as long as it had. His last patient left that afternoon around 4:30 p.m. He contemplated whether to go home early or finish developing a program for families in his grief counseling group, when the phone rang. He could not have prepared himself for the story about to be to him by the women on the other end of the line.

"Hello, Josh Stewart, please," said Lizzy in her most professional voice.

"This is Josh."

Lizzy didn't know where to start. She paused and suddenly felt stymied.

"Hello?" Josh repeated.

"Hello," Lizzy stuttered, "My name is Lizzy Sterling and I've had a strange experience over the last month. What I'm about to say is going to sound crazy so I was hoping you would be willing to hear me out before passing judgment. A couple of friends and I would like to meet with you so we can accomplish a task that has inadvertently become our responsibility."

"Well, shoot," said Josh, his curiosity peaked.

"Through a strange set of circumstances," Lizzy paused before she launched into what she felt was sure to be a sensitive area for Josh, "I have had, or rather a couple friends that I work with have been contacted by your....sister."

There was silence for what seemed like a lifetime. Josh was so taken off guard he didn't know how to respond.

"My sister is dead Miss. She died 20 years ago. You must be mistaken."

"Mr. Stewart, I am aware that your sister has passed. What I'm telling you, I am sure sounds crazy, but she has contacted several people over the last few weeks. I have a friend who is a sensitive or rather a psychic. She has been able to decipher and receive a message from Sunday. Unfortunately, Sunday has demanded that a certain person bring the message to you personally."

"I don't know who you are, but I have to tell you I don't appreciate this!" Josh said sternly. *Who does this? Is this some sick joke?* he thought, waiting for Lizzy's response.

Lizzy stayed calm and focused.

"Mr. Stewart, I know this must sound unbelievable but please hear me out. The home you lived in, where your sister passed, has been haunted with her spirit for twenty years. My girlfriend lives a couple of streets over from the house. Her children are friends with the girl and boy who currently reside there. They told my friend's son that they were scared and there was paranormal activity in their house. This information, however, came after one of the children had visited my friend's house. Shortly after this visit, my friend began to experience strange activity in her home. She had lived there for two years and never had anything like this happen. I went to her home to do a blessing and see if we could clear the spirit out of her house. The ceremony seemed to have worked as she hadn't had any activity for a few weeks. Then a week ago, her daughter's friend called her to say she was frightened and that there was odd activity occurring at her triplex.

Two other housemates confirmed having some kind of paranormal experience as well. It had apparently attached to this girl when she was visiting my friend. It then appeared, that Sunday, attached herself to the boy who lives next door in the triplex and traveled home with him. I am no 'Ghostbuster' sir, this simply started because I was trying to help a friend. I'm now neck deep into something, which honestly, I feel I need to see it through to its conclusion. I am calling you because your sister, Sunday, made her wishes clear to my friend, the psychic. She has a message for you and she will not transcend, move into the light that is, until she imparts this message to you." Lizzy paused; silence filled the uncomfortable seconds. "She is a trapped soul! I now feel a responsibility to get her where she needs to go, and to do that you must agree to meet with us."

"Give me your number," Josh snapped. "I will have to call you back."

Lizzy reeled off her cell number and emphasized before hanging up, "Your sister is stuck. She wants contact with you and the sooner we meet the better."

"I will call you back," Josh repeated firmly and hung up.

Josh sat in silence for a long time. He ran the terrible hours of that day shortly after his 12th birthday over in his mind. He had messed around after school and had gotten home a little later than normal. When he arrived, he found Sunday on the couch. He thought she was sleeping and snuck up to scare her. He grabbed her shoulder and yelled, "Boo!" in her ear but she didn't move.

"Sunday?" he said as he shook her shoulder. "Sunday!" he yelled. She still didn't move. "This isn't funny!" he said loudly in her ear. She still didn't move. He turned her over and her blue lips seemed to leap off her face. He panicked but managed to run to the phone and called 911. The 911 operator asked, "Is she breathing?" Josh pulled her over accidently pulling her to the floor.

Josh screamed into the phone, "her lips are blue, her lips are blue!" He laid his head on her chest but heard nothing. "No heartbeat! Please get someone here now!" he screamed the tears rolling down his cheeks.

Josh loved his big sister. Of course, they had their sibling moments but she was a kind girl and always protective of Josh. He held her in his lap and lightly smoothed her forehead with his hand. The paramedics burst through the front door to find a sorry scene of a young boy cradling his dead sister in his arms.

"Her lips are blue," is all he would say.

His parents were called and they met him at the hospital, but it was too late, their daughter was dead. The doctors told his parents that Sunday had been dead for over an hour by the time Josh found Sunday. He could never quite let himself off the hook, feeling he could have stopped her. Even though the doctor assured him he could not have saved her, even had he come home earlier, Josh could not stop blaming himself. All these years later, he still could not figure how he missed the signs of his 'suicidal' sister. She had not been a depressed girl. Popular and loved she should have lived a long happy life. It was damn Tom Hoskins. He loved her and left her. He jilted her and never had the courage to tell her he was done with her. Josh remembered one of his favorite 'kill Tom' fantasy's and smiled.

The devastation of his sister's death was swift. The family moved within a month of her death. Josh knew his parents tried to be strong for him but he could see the strain and the sadness that permeated their lives. The weight of the grief they felt was unbearable at times. The new knowledge that anything can happen, at any time, and can level the life you know, was a lot for a twelve year old to handle. Frankly, it was a lot for his parents to handle.

Josh's experience definitely enhanced his sensitivity as a therapist. He picked up gentle nuances of people who were a danger to themselves. He didn't know how many clients he had talked off the ledge or even just put a spotlight on what they were thinking of doing. He helped his clients reframe their lives before they did something that they could never take back. It wasn't that he didn't believe in an afterlife, but this 'out of the blue' call threw him for a loop. He couldn't imagine someone just making up a story like this to torture him.

The dull colors of dusk pushed across the horizon. He looked at the round clock on the wall and was surprised it was already 6:30 p.m. Cynthia would be home by now. He rolled his eyes and sighed, *There is no way I'm telling her about any of this*!

Lizzy stopped by Karen's for a pep talk that encouraged her to finally make the call to Josh.

"Uhm, I could tell he was thoroughly annoyed or thought I was a crazy."

"He's a therapist, he'll get over it. We know what we experienced. It's not our fault we've met up with some ghost with a mission," Karen said, trying to help Lizzy feel better. She knew she wouldn't have been able to make the call.

"It appears from the research I've been doing that most spirits or earth bound ghosts, who are still on the earth plane, have a mission. In a way, they are stuck, some by choice, some by confusion," Lizzy said. She felt genuinely sad about the plight of the souls who were stuck in between life and the light. She believed she might be able to help them with their unfinished business.

"Alright," said Karen, "you are doing what she asked, so stop this brooding."

"What if he doesn't call back? Will Sunday go on a rampage at Tom and Deanna's house?"

"This has been a long few weeks, you're doing the best you can," said Karen.

Lizzy suddenly jumped up, paced around the room to push down her panic.

"What if I'm not doing the best I can do? She said, arms flailing. "I don't even know WHAT I'm doing. I thought I had done a successful blessing on your house. I've realized I haven't done or been successful at anything. I've blessed two houses that didn't even have a spirit in them. Who knows if I even have one clue about how to be successful at any of this. I've basically been blessing an empty box!" she rolled her eyes, shook her head and continued to stomp around the room. "Technically, I'm a failure."

"That is so much crap!" said Karen.

Lizzy could feel her defeat and couldn't shake it. Thank God for Karen's cooking. It always made Lizzy feel better so it wasn't hard for Karen to convince Lizzy to stay for dinner. Karen did her best to distract her from her worries. The hours passed and Lizzy concluded he wasn't calling back.

"It's him!" Lizzy said excited and surprised.

"Hello?"

"Ok, I'll meet with you," Josh's deep voice was clear and concise. "We can meet here at my office if you'd like."

"Thank you," said Lizzy deeply relieved. "It will have to be after 6:00 p,m. if it is during the week or we can set a time on the weekend as we are an hour away. There will be four of us." Lizzy saw Karen out of the corner of her eye shaking her head and mouthing the word "No".

"I told you I'm not going this time Lizzy," Karen hissed from the Kitchen.

"Ok, no, three of us," Lizzy corrected hastily.

"That's fine. The address is 1475 Walnut St.," Josh said. "Josh, there is one more thing I need to tell you. Tom Hoskins will be with us at your sister's request. She asked him to find you, meet with you and confirm what has happened."

"I don't want to see that jackass!" Josh yelled. Then just as quickly, as that outburst flew from his mouth, he quickly changed gears and muttered, "No, wait, maybe I do want to see that jackass."

"What time?" asked Lizzy, glad that he agreed to see Tom.

"How about 7:00 pm Thursday," Josh replied.

"That should work but I will need to confirm with the rest of my group. How about pencil us in and I will be able to get back to you by tomorrow evening."

Thursday arrived and Lizzy's plan started out well. Lizzy pulled up to Tom's house at 6:45 p.m., beeped the horn twice and waited for Tom who slowly stepped out of house giving the impression that he was non to excited for the trip a head. Janet nudged Lizzy, "He's a really nice looking man, isn't he?"

"Yes," Lizzy agreed, "lucky us."

"Hello, how are you?" Lizzy asked Tom while he settled into the seat.

"I don't want to do this but I am, I am."

"That's kind of obvious," said Janet. She turned and looked into his worried eyes, "Tom, it will be fine."

Lizzy pulled away from the curb feeling a thousand butterflies in her stomach. She hoped that once Sunday knew her brother had gotten her message that she would move toward the light. She prayed there would be clear direction. She didn't have a clue how it would all work out or if she had what it took to help Sunday cross over. She would just have to have faith and take her cues from Janet and Sunday.

It struck Lizzy as strange that Josh's office was only five miles from Tom's house. It also seemed odd they had never crossed paths in all these years Josh had been back in the area.

Janet broke the silence, "Sunday is with us, you all know that right?"

"No," both Tom and Lizzy said at the same time.

"Well, she is," said Janet. "She is still attached to Tom."

Tom looked around the backseat as though he might see Sunday. He felt chilled and rubbed his arms wanting to feel more comfortable. He had caught a faint hint of her perfume that morning but didn't notice anything else. It felt a little strange to think of Sunday being attached to him and even traveling with him.

"Sunday is in low energy right now and is preparing to see her brother. She is saving her energy for their meeting," with that, Janet turned in her seat and kept quiet the remainder of the ride.

Lizzy reached their destination and parked in front of a quaint brick building with the sign *Sunday's Song Counseling Center.* A tall, well built, dark haired man with a goatee walked out the door. His eyes caught Lizzy's eyes and he smiled. *This must be him*, Lizzy thought. She noticed he and Tom were about the same size.

Lizzy turned to Janet, "We're in the land of the giants."

"It appears we are," Janet responded with a giggle.

Lizzy stepped out of the car first. "Hello, Josh?"

He waved as he approached the car. His blue eyes locked onto Lizzy's for a brief moment. She felt her heart kick up a notch. Whose wouldn't, the man was something to behold. Tom came around the back end of the car and took three steps onto the grass toward Josh. Josh's attention moved from Lizzy to Tom. Tom nervously approached Josh with a smile and his hand out ready to shake Josh's hand. Before Lizzy, or any of them knew what was happening, Josh launched himself onto Tom, tackling him to the ground. The two men rolled on the ground grunting.

"Holy shit! No Josh, please don't!" Lizzy screamed as she rushed toward the two fighting men.

Janet caught Lizzy by the arm and jerked her back.

"You're not getting in the middle of that, are you crazy?" said Janet.

Josh yelled out, "You're gonna finally get what you deserve you bastard!"

Tom stopped and protected his face with both arms as Josh straddled him with raised fists.

"Just do it and get it over with!" bellowed Tom.

Josh caught a glimpse of Lizzy and Janet's horrified faces and paused. The red fiery rage pulsing through him, paused just long enough for Josh to realize what he had done. He appeared confused for a moment and then lowered his fists.

"God, I'm sorry Tom!" he boomed as he pushed himself up to a standing position and held his hand out to help Tom up.

"I kind of had it comin' Josh," Tom said as he scrambled to his feet, brushing himself off.

Lizzy, without thinking, threw her hand out to Josh and blurted out "I'm Lizzy!" Everything had happened so fast, she was flustered. Lizzy locked on to Josh's deep blue eyes again and couldn't help but noticed the handsome face beneath the dark goatee. Josh managed and smile as his big hand encompassed Lizzy's.

"Hello, Lizzy. I'm sorry about that." He looked back at Tom and shook his head. "I'm not sure what came over me, I saw him get out of the car and I just kind of lost it. Through the years I have planned a thousand ways to kill you Tom, but I wasn't serious."

Janet stood quiet as a mouse wondering if the fireworks were over.

"This is Janet," Lizzy said, "she's the level headed one of the group!"

"Pleased to meet you, level headed Janet," Josh said, motioning them to follow him to the office.

"Let's get off the street. I hope no one else saw me brawling in front of my counseling center. It certainly gives off a completely different impression then I've intended for my business! I can see a commercial now, 'Come to Sunday's Song Counseling Center, open up to me and I'll kick your ass until r I'll kick your ass until you do.' I'm pretty sure that won't be a huge draw for clients." He could not believe he had reacted so spontaneously and aggressively. He hadn't realized that the anger he had for Tom was still so hot!

The office had been tastefully decorated with earth tone colors and calming landscape paintings on the walls. Josh led them into the 'Family' room. The large room, painted sage green with white trim held a large circle of chairs in the middle of it. This is where Josh held his group sessions with grieving families. The chairs were sturdy with good comfortable cushions.

It's a nice touch, Lizzy thought, *to make things as comfortable as possible for families while they get their heads shrunk.* Lizzy laughed to herself. Josh pulled four chairs into an inner circle for them to meet.

Lizzy began relaying the events of the past weeks from her perspective. She turned the floor over to Tom who then detailed his paranormal weekend.

"That's about it," said Tom. "I figured out the writing on the mirror was 'Josh Now' right when I saw it. Janet made it very clear that Sunday wants to connect with you. I figured I could find you and the truth is, I owe Sunny."

"It's quite a story," Josh said as he pondered everything that was said. As unbelievable as it seemed, there were three people sitting in his office who believed emphatically that the events had taken place just as portrayed.

"I'm still not sure where I stand on all of this, so what is it that you want to do next?" asked Josh.

Janet, who had been very quiet, spoke with authority, "I need a few minutes of silence. I felt Sunday very strongly in the car and I know she is attached to Tom. She showed me, or impressed images or thoughts upon me regarding her death. She insisted that she see you before she could move on. I need to see if I can still connect with her as deeply as I did last weekend."

Janet shut her eyes and quieted her mind. She sensed Sunday's energy move next to Josh. She was just about to speak, when the air around them became noticeably colder, and the distinct smell of Loves Baby Soft perfume erupted into the room.

Josh stood up so quickly he knocked his chair over. He scanned the room in alarm.

Janet calmly moved toward him, "It's ok, please sit down." She motioned with her hand for him to sit back down.

"That perfume. She was wearing that the day she died. I'll never forget it," said Tom softly.

"Yes," Janet kneeled down in front of Josh and held his hand, "she wants you to know she is here."

A tear trickled down his cheek and onto the floor.

Sunday had been living in a strange afterworld for over 25 years. In her mind, she was still 16 and her brother was 12. She sensed the energy from his soul which is timeless but also could see he was a grown man.

The day she died, her spirit sat next to Josh and tried to let him know she was there, safe and sound. He was so distraught she refused to leave his side. She had been very confused by what she saw and experienced the day she died. She saw her lifeless body lying in Josh's lap, but also found herself sitting next to him. She tried to console him but nothing seemed to work. She

106

screamed at him hoping her message would permeate his mind and let him know or feel that she was not dead. He could not hear her. She could still think, perceive and move around; she wanted Josh to know it. He couldn't feel her presence at the time with all the adrenalin pumping through his veins. His sister lay dead and the grief surrounded him like a black cloud.

Sunday had strange dream-like memories of her first few months after her death. She became very frustrated trying to reach her loved ones. She kept trying to communicate with her family with no response. She remembered the grief energy in the house being so thick and sad that she wanted to escape but found there was no doorway out. She had tried to let them know she was safe but she didn't know then how to use her energy in the spirit world.

Then, one day, they were gone. She realized the house was empty and their energy was gone, just like that. How could they just leave her? Over the next twenty five years, several families moved in and out of the house. After about a year, she found she was able to manipulate lights and create the aroma of her perfume. A few years after that, she was able to create a knock. That was her favorite ability because it got the most attention.

When Sunday realized that she could be heard, she really focused on getting noticed. Eventually, she was able to remove pictures from the walls, open cabinet doors and pull drawers out. She found manipulating drawers, cabinet doors, and faucets, had proven to be quite difficult and took a lot of energy. She had to build up her energy for quite some time before she could move objects. She found she could draw off the electrical system in the house. She got a real kick out of scaring the new homeowners. The came and they went.

Then, about two years ago, a family moved in and the son, Ben, was quite psychically sensitive. Ben reminded her of Josh. He responded to her presence every time she was near. He was a funny awkward teenage boy and she loved every inch of him. She pined for Josh but utilized Ben as a substitute because the house had become her prison.

Over time, Sunday found that gathering energy came more easily. There were so many electronics in the house. In some ways, it was an energy smorgasbord. She learned to speak his name and sometimes he heard her, to Sunday's absolute glee. It gave her hope that she might be able to communicate at some point and maybe even be able to find a way to reach her family.

Sunday hadn't meant to scare Ben. There were others that she took great delight in scaring but Ben was not one of them. One day she found him crying in his room after she had been doing some knocking near his bed. She hoped that maybe a doorway of communication might be opened. When he got up to leave the room, she followed him wanting to soothe him. She became very focused and began trying again, to reach into his mind. She hadn't noticed he was walking out the front door. When she did realize what he was doing, she panicked, and instinctually she reached into his aura and found herself stuck to him. She rode right out the door with him. What a fantastic surprise! She had not been outside the house in 25 years!

Ben rode his bike to a nice little house a few streets away to collect for his paper route and get his mind off his haunting. When he arrived there, a boy he called Billy, answered the door and invited them inside. She liked Billy, he looked to be about 12 years old and again, it made her long for Josh. When walked to the door to leave, she reached out and touched Billy's aura and 'bing' she was attached to Billy like magic.

Sunday found that Billy's whole family was quite sensitive. The discovery that she could leave her house gave her knew hope that she might be able to find her brother. She had learned how to ramp up her energy and she did pull some antics at Karen's house.

Old habits die hard, she thought.

She did feel bad when she sensed their fear but she had a mission and could not let their fear get in her way. Giddy with the possibility of finding someone who she might be able to communicate with, Sunday settled in at Karen's. When Tina arrived at Karen's house for dinner, Sunday felt uncontrollably drawn to her. Once again, she touched Tina's aura as she was leaving the house and 'bing' again, out the door she went.

As far as Sunday was concerned, Tina had the worst taste in music. Fortunately, Sunday found she could change the radio station with ease and moved the station to one of her liking. Sunday often lost track of time and wasn't sure how long she had been at the triplex. She had been diligently attempting to get someone's attention. She projected sounds into every room of the triplex. Someone heard her, didn't they? Her frustration began to balloon until the day Greg knocked on Tina's door. His energy seemed familiar, she couldn't explain it. She didn't know what it was exactly, but she decided she liked him better than Tina and jumped right onto his aura.

Greg reacted poorly to her 'operation smell me' tactic and when he turned on his heels to leave the apartment, she almost missed the chance to get out the door with him. She was proud of herself though. When he arrived at his parent's house you could have pushed her over with a feather. *No, a feather was still too dense and would have gone right through her*, she thought. When Tom walked into the room, Sunday couldn't believe it. She recognized his soul energy immediately. She also noticed he was quite a bit older than she remembered. He certainly was no less attractive by any stretch of the imagination. In fact, she had thought maybe even more attractive! How long had she been locked in that house? She lamented her situation, and how it came to be.

Then his wife walked in and Sunday had those old fleshy thoughts of jealously rise up into her energy field. *What could it all mean that she ended up at Tom's house of all places? Was it the light? Was it drawing her in? Was it guiding her so she could finish her need to comfort her brother? Would she finally be able to move on?* All these questions and more ran through her soul.

She didn't pretend to understand. For the next 24 hours or so she had a lot of fun creating havoc in that house. As soon as he smelled her perfume, she knew she had him! When he pulled the tattered obituary out of his wallet and apologized to what he thought was the air…she felt the impact of his guilt and grief. No, that was not what she was after. Twenty five years ago, yes, she wanted to get his attention and make him feel bad for how he had let her down. She wanted him to feel the pain she felt when she saw the wedding announcement in the paper. *How could he have been so callous? Things become clearer when you shed the thing we call a body*, she thought. She realized that Tom had carried a burden for many years and it wasn't entirely fair. Yes, he had been a total jackass. He was young. She, however, was the one who made the decision to take the pills. She didn't know at the time how the drugs in the cabinet were to be used. Some were her father's, some were her mother's prescriptions and the cocktail she created was legendary.

When Sunday saw the local paper displaying Tom and Deanna's wedding announcement her heart broke. *What's the worst that could happen?* She had thought as she poured a handful of pills into her hand. She gulped them down with one big swish. *Stomach pumped*, she thought, *that would be the worst part.*

Her parents would completely freak out. She figured she would get a lot of one-on-one attention after this escapade. It was all about Tom though. Sunday fantasized that as she lay in her hospital bed Tom would rush to her side and apologize. He would realize how much she loved him and would dump that bitch. Sunday would be Mrs. Tom Hoskins.

Sunday's fantasy didn't play out the way she planned. The cocktail she mixed that afternoon was a potent little concoction. She also didn't know that she was very sensitive to drugs in general. She went to sleep and the next thing she knew, she was kneeling next to her brother, looking at her own body, lying in his lap. What had she done? She was mortified when she realized she was dead. There was no getting back into that body. She tried. No one could hear her. Those first few months were very frightening. After she had accepted what had happened, another blow came when her family moved out of the house. Where was she when they did that? Why hadn't she noticed the hustle and bustle of moving? She never understood it. Over the years, she missed her family intensely and she never forgot the distraught 12 year old boy who had tried in vain to revive her. *Poor Josh! How had all this affected him?* She wondered.

When Josh came out the office door and charged Tom, she, like everyone, was surprised. She was still attached to Tom's aura and when he went down, she went down with him. She stared disbelievingly into the 38-year-old eyes of her brother. She read his energy but was stunned by his age and size. *Look at HIM! He has turned out to be quite a man* she thought. *Mom was right, all that baby fat was preparing him for some Paul Bunion growth spurt.* Had she been in human form she wasn't sure she would have recognized him. As a spirit though, she saw his energy immediately and she felt all the love she had always felt for her brother. It was overwhelming.

As angry as she was that day she took those pills, now she was not angry. All that tangled energy was gone. She didn't want to hurt Tom or Deanna. She did enjoy the torment she had created over that first weekend with him, but thrill quickly wore off. She could deeply feel his sadness and his pain. It had created a dark spot in his aura and for that, she was sorry.

He could have handled things better in the past but he didn't. The bottom line was that his immature actions should not have been a life sentence. *Kids do stupid things. Young men...do stupid things.* Sunday mulled it all over and over for twenty five long years.

Now, here they all were in the same room. *Together again,* laughed Sunday. She knelt down in front of her brother and saw the tear run down his cheeks. She felt his loss and grief so acutely she wanted to fly out of the room. This was precisely why she needed to see him. It was for some of the same reasons she needed to reconnect with Tom as well. It was important that she release them from their bondage and then she felt she could finally be free to move on.

Janet relaxed and did the best she could to connect with Sunday and avoid getting tangled in Josh's sadness. She found the task difficult.

Sunday began projecting information with all her might. She hoped Janet would receive the transmission.

Janet looked into Josh's sad eyes, "Josh, she is showing me a picture of a, uhm, a Gremlin?"

Josh sat straight up in his chair and nodded in disbelief.

"She is showing me an image of a movie title and a dog. She is letting me know that you watched the movie, Gremlins?" Janet paused as she put together images she didn't quite know how to interpret, then continued, "You watched Gremlins many, many, she is saying with a deep sigh, many times."

"Yes," said Josh transfixed on Janet's eyes, "It was my favorite movie when I was about seven. I made Sunny watch it no less than twenty times."

Janet continued, "She is showing me a small dog. Sunday is pointing to a sign with a picture of water with a big red 'X' over the top of it. I have no idea what it means."

Slowly a smile crept across Josh's face, "I wouldn't let my Mother wash our Shih Tzu. I had convinced myself he was a Mogwai and would cause a lot of Gremlin havoc if he got wet!" He laughed heartily as the memories came flooding back like it was yesterday.

"She wants to know that you believe she is here," said Janet.

"I do believe she is here," said Josh.

Janet sat quiet for what seemed like a very long time. "Josh, she is so sorry for what she put you through. It was an accident. She truly believed she would be fine and at worst, would end up in the hospital getting her stomach pumped. She had a fantasy that Tom would rush to her side and take her back."

Tom gasped and put his head into his hands. "Damn it Sunny!" he whispered to himself.

"Josh, she wants you to know how much she loves you and your parents. She wants you to tell them she is ok, no, that she is great. She is getting very intense now Josh. She needs you to understand there was NOTHING you could have done to save her.

She messed up, not you. Please let this go and allow love and joy into your life."

Josh looked confused, "I understand."

"No," said Janet very intently, looking directly into his eyes and grabbing his broad shoulders, "Josh, this was not your fault. You must begin to let love and joy into your life. She said you have resisted. She is telling me you are not happy and she knows it's because of her; it's because of what happened. You must re-evaluate your life and find how you can…live!"

Janet standing now, walked to the middle of the room. "This is so important that both you men understand that she is sorry. She wants your forgiveness so she can move on."

Tom spoke first as he wiped his eyes, "She wants my forgiveness? That is ridiculous after how I hurt her and created all this misery?"

"No Tom, you must forgive yourself. She does not hold you responsible. She forgives your adolescent action and is asking that you forgive yourself and her for what she did."

"Josh, can you forgive her?" Lizzy finally spoke.

"Of course I can!"

"Can you forgive yourself?" asked Janet.

Silence dropped over the room. Both men sat in their chairs, drained. Neither knew how to forgive themselves at that moment.

Agitated, Sunday pushed a picture off the wall. The sudden crash jolted everyone in the room.

Janet paced around the room. She could feel Sunday's frustration. Sunday had been pondering all this for the last 25 years. She was ready to move into the light.

"The two of you are blocking her path!" Janet quickly raised her voice. Both men looked up at Janet not knowing how to transition from 25 years of guilt and shame to forgiveness.

"Well, these are Sunday's words not mine," Janet said as she delivered the rest of the message, "For such big strong guys, you're a couple pussies! She said she is the one who is dead. Get over it! You're alive, start living!"

Tom weary from the weight of Sunday's death in his life wanted to let it go. He was ready and began to pray.

Janet's head snapped around to look at Tom, "Forgive yourself and tell her if you forgive her."

"I definitely forgive her!" said Tom as he shifted in his chair.

"Now Josh," said Janet, "she is quite intense about this. She will kick your ass to Texas if you don't let loose of this self-loathing!

Sunday pushed as hard as she could and tried to touched Josh's face and kiss his forehead. At that moment, he felt her. He completely felt her and he understood. "I forgive her, I forgive myself," Josh said, wiping the tears from his face as 25 years of grief and self-blame lifted from his soul.

"Heal thyself, counselor," Josh said out loud.

"Let's join hands and see if we can help send her into the light," Lizzy said as she gathered Tom's and Josh's hands in hers.

The four stood in a circle holding hands and praying for Sunday. Sunday was ready to move on. The light had been calling her for some time, but she had been ignoring it. Now that she had made right what she believed was her wrong, she could go now. The group helped send her off with their thoughts and prayers. Sunday Stewart, after 25 years of lingering in the gap between worlds, moved into a bright, warm, loving light. She felt complete love as she disappeared off this earth plane.

"She's gone," said Janet.

Lizzy nodded her head, "I felt it too!"

The group stood silent for a moment. It wasn't every day you moved someone from one existence to another. The room felt lighter. Lizzy and Janet hugged Tom and Josh. Josh and Tom looked at each other for a moment and then embraced. Lizzy noticed that both men looked a bit younger and lighter in their energy.

Lizzy handed Tom and Josh her card with her and Janet's phone numbers. "Just in case you run into something else or just need someone to talk to. I have found that not everyone is open to hearing about supernatural events."

"This is going to take a little time to process," Josh said as he ushered everyone into the foyer. "I've never experienced anything like this. I felt her, I really felt her in there."

Out at the curb they gave each other one last hug and departed. Josh stood at the curb and watched them drive away. He wasn't exactly sure what he felt but a great sense of relief and a feeling of joy percolated in his broad chest. The weight of Sunday's death freshly off his chest made him want to celebrate her life and his. He called Cynthia and told her to get her best dress on, they were going out!

Lizzy and Janet dropped Tom off at his home. The girls got out of the car with him and walked him to his door.

"Are you ok?" Janet asked.

"I am. This has been a very odd experience. As Josh said, it will take some time to process. I can say I do feel lighter. I didn't realize just how much this has weighed me down all these years. I fell in love with my wife. I never meant to hurt Sunday the way I did. I realize now, that although I have been very happy in my marriage, this has been a dark cloud existing within me all these years. I look forward to moving on without it. Thank you so much for your help." Tom stepped forward and hugged Janet and then Lizzy.

"If you need us for anything, please don't hesitate to call," said Lizzy.

"I will. You girls drive carefully and good luck in your future endeavors. If I hear of someone who needs a Ghost Investigator I'll give them your names."

"We're not ghost investigators!" laughed Lizzy. "We just wanted to help my friend Karen and it turned into this whole other thing!"

"Well, it appears you ARE some kind of spirit workers so, like I said, if I hear of anything I will send them your way. Smiling he turned around and gave a back handed wave as he strode through his front door. Lizzy and Janet could hear Greg and Deanna inside asking him a hundred questions about what happened. The door shut and Lizzy and Janet began their journey home.

CHAPTER 16

Lizzy and Janet talked fast and furious on their way home. They reviewed every detail of what had happened.

"I think it went very well," said Janet, grinning ear to ear.

"So, what do you think? Should we become the next GI's?" asked Lizzy with a smirk.

"GI's?" Janet didn't put it together.

"You know, Ghost Investigators," Lizzy laughed. "I feel we could be of real help to people. You know, maybe it was lucky all this happened as it did. What would have happened if Sunday had attached to someone else and had found her way to Tom somehow? Tom and his wife might have dealt with a lot of paranormal activity for a long time before they would have gotten help and Sunday may have been stuck here for a really long time."

"So, what? You want to advertise?" said Janet apprehensively.

"I don't know about all that," Lizzy said as her excitement started to build. "Yes, to a degree maybe we should. I mean we could put a little website up and just let people know what we are up to. What would it be like to help lead other trapped spirits to the light? It feels good doesn't it?"

"It does have an interestingly happy energy to it. It was a little stressful getting there though. I don't know that I will always connect as well as I did this time. I can't be expected to perform on cue you know," Janet said.

"I think between the two of us we will be able to get enough information and it will be fine. If we don't, we don't. All we can do is be willing to be of service. We set our intention to be of help and see where it leads us. I've noticed on a lot of these TV programs, the paranormal investigators go in and seem to just stir things up. Many times, they leave the people with the problem. Sometimes the paranormal activity actually gets worse after they leave. The people getting haunted have no idea what to do. We could contact some of these teams and let them know we can cleanse the homes and maybe even get more information for them," Lizzy's mind raced like a freight train with ideas. As always, she would land on an idea, or cause, and become completely consumed by it. She couldn't help herself. She felt that it was something she wanted, or maybe even needed to do. There seemed to be a force behind it pulling her in.

"I'm in," said Janet. "How many ghostly issues could there be out there anyway?"

CHAPTER 17

Karen waited on pins and needles for Lizzy to arrive. She flew out the door to meet her when Lizzy pulled into the driveway.

"Well, how was it? Were you scared? Did she get her message out? Did her brother believe you?"

"Whoa there, hundred question Nellie! Give me a chance to answer the first question before you hammer me with three more!" Lizzy said as she put her arm around Karen and started into the house. "What did you cook me for dinner? I'm totally starved!"

"Roast beef, baby!" Karen said with a giggle "Before I make you tell me everything though, there is something I have to tell you," she said with a big Cheshire cat grin.

"My God, what?" Lizzy could only imagine at this point, what Karen had going. This had been one crazy month.

Karen pulled a card out of her pocket and handed it to Lizzy. "Just in case you lost it, 'Officer Dan' would like you to call him."

"Whhhat!" Lizzy squealed. "He came here?"

"He sure did. He asked me to please pass a message to you that he would like to take you to dinner. He also asked me to remind you to be mindful when dressing because where he is taking you requires all clothing to be worn right side out. He plans on taking you somewhere nice," Karen said, beaming now. It wasn't often that a man tracked Lizzy down for a date and this one most certainly, romantically, did.

Lizzy rolled her eyes and stuffed the card in her pocket, "This is all just too much. Feed me and let me tell you what happened, I'll deal with lover boy later."

Lizzy gave every detail to Karen. She finished the story and her dinner at the same time. Emotionally exhausted and physically stuffed, she had to go home and get into bed.

"That was an amazing dinner buddy, thank you. I need to head out though. I'm so tired right now I can barely stand myself," Lizzy sat on the edge of the couch not wanting to eat and run but she was spent. She had been so energized earlier and in one fell swoop, she felt completely drained. "I've got to go get some sleep."

"Its fine," Karen laughed. "Before you go I have to talk to you about two things. First, I won't be joining you on any further, whatever you call them, ghost chasings."

"I'm surprised," said Lizzy. "I thought when I told you Janet agreed to proceed I kind of just assumed you would be there as well. Why don't you want to be a part of this?" asked Lizzy.

Karen breathed deep that drew a long sigh, "I just don't want to. There is too much drama. You know, Sunday wasn't in your house banging around, she was in mine. It was upsetting. Even though I know now that she was trying to get attention so she could get some help getting to the other side, I didn't enjoy it.

"That's true," Lizzy admitted.

"All my life I have heard of haunted houses, but I never heard of haunted people. I think that is what we experienced in this situation. If the spirit of Sunday Stewart was able to attach itself to someone and travel, then other spirits can do the same thing. It was eye-opening, that's for sure. I've decided I don't want to take a chance of bringing something back into my home."

"I know, but we can protect ourselves now. We know how to move them out of the house and to the other side," Lizzy said suddenly feeling abandoned.

"No, Lizzy we don't know any of that for sure. We didn't really cleanse my house of a spirit as we thought because she had already left."

"You're right. I do feel we can protect ourselves though," Lizzy moved into sales pitch mode. She didn't want to do this without Karen.

"Lizzy, don't. I can see in your eyes you want to convince me. I have kids and I am not taking any chances. Billy was being traumatized and I didn't know it. That is a terrible feeling. These spirits are single minded and motivated when they are trying to finish their mission. I don't want to be in between them and their mission."

"All right! All right!" Lizzy bellowed, throwing her hands in the air. She refused to hide her disappointment. She knew when Karen set her mind to something that was it. She was even more stubborn than Lizzy.

"Now, on to a happier topic!" Karen said jumping up and grabbing Lizzy's belongings. "You go home, call that Officer Dan and then get some sleep, you look like shit!"

"Thanks," Lizzy said sarcastically. She waved Karen off. "I'll think about it. It sounds like a lot of trouble."

"Lizzy, you call him. He came all the way, over here chasing you down! It's very romantic."

"Oh shut up!" Lizzy couldn't get out of Karen's clutches fast enough. "I will call him! Don't go buying us wedding china or anything else, geez!"

Lizzy arrived home, parked her car and walked straight into her bedroom. She tore off her clothes and jumped into bed without even brushing her teeth. She didn't care, she felt delirium setting in. Her head hit the pillow and she was gone.

Friday, at work, she could not concentrate. Had she really helped Sunday cross over? Lizzy felt strange and oddly gratified, she believed they had done something really meaningful for those families. Sitting at her desk, thumbing through the invoices she needed to mail out now seemed…stupid.

She worked for System Gifts for four years. The job paid the bills. Lizzy could sell. She always managed to make a good living but this company to one degree or another seemed 'soul-less'. There seemed to be no real meaning to the trinkets and traveler's mementos Lizzy promoted.

There is a whole other world and dimension going on around us. Souls are working to finish unfinished business and maybe I can help. Lizzy thought, as she restacked the invoices she had stacked just a moment ago. Her mind writhed around trying to process everything she had been exposed to the last few weeks. She picked up her phone and returned calls to her clients. Lizzy knew she wasn't going to get much done today. She pushed the business card around on her desk with 'Officer Dan's' phone number displayed with a red circle prominently around it.

Oh why not, she asked herself. She took a moment to gather her courage and then dialed his number. Why was she feeling so nervous? It's not like she'd never gone on a date for God's sake. The line rang. Her stomach jumped into her throat. She swallowed hard and waited as the phone rang a second time. She started to hang up when he answered.

"This is Dan," said a smooth voice on the other end of the line.

"Hello, this is Lizzy Sterling. We met at my friend Karen's house a few weeks back. She said you stopped by. She told me to call you." Her words came out like machine gun fire.

"Lizzy! Hello! I'm so glad you called me," Dan said with an obvious smile in his voice.

"Well here I am. What is it that you want?" She tried to cover up how nervous this made her but it just made everything she said blunt than she meant to be. *I am such a tool when it comes to men and dating,* she thought.

Dan burst out laughing, "I would like to invite you to dinner if you'd consider going."

"Hmm, well I do need to eat sometimes so I suppose I could do that. When were you thinking?"

"How about Friday at 7:00 p.m.?" said Dan.

"Today is Friday."

"I meant next Friday," said Dan.

Oh no, she thought. *There is no getting out of a Friday night 'horror date' because you can't make a good excuse about getting up early for work.*

"I can't Friday," Lizzy lied. "I'm busy this whole week except Thursday, I could do Thursday."

"Thursday it is then. Will 7 o'clock work for you? I'd like to take you to the Royal Crown."

"Oh?" She had to think if she even owned anything appropriate to wear. The Royal Crown, known as the most expensive, hoity-toity restaurant in town, had a dress code, formal. She had only been there twice. She had been there once after she graduated from college and more recently for a wedding reception. She wondered why someone would want to take her there for a first date. It seemed a little pretentious. She had been adventurous all month, so she decided to go for it even though she'd have to find a dress.

"Alright, 7:00 p.m. will be fine. Are you picking me up or am I meeting you there?" she asked pointedly.

"Wow! Who have you been dating?" Dan asked as he laughed openly again. "I will pick you up if you will trust me with your address."

"3700 Spiker Lane. I'm right down from Landis Park."

"I know where it is, I'll see you then."

"See you then," she quickly hung up. *Thank God that was over*! She called Karen immediately.

"Well, I called him, are you happy now?" she sighed loudly.

"Oh my God! Tell me everything! When are you going? Where are you going? And stop sounding so put out!" Karen knew that Lizzy got nervous on dates, about dates and about men in general. Karen was a romantic and she just knew the right man

123

was out there for Lizzy. Lizzy needed to put herself out there and stop being so serious all the time.

"I need a dress. He's taking me to the Royal Crown."

"Oh my God! Oh my God!" repeated Karen.

"Oh my God is right! Calm down. I think he'd been better off to ask you out," Lizzy's insecurities began spilling out. How was it that she could feel so strong one minute, so optimistic, and the thought of going out with a man pulled the rug completely out from under her?

"Do you want to go shopping or see what I have in my closet?" Karen asked excitedly.

"Let's take a look at what you have first. Do you think you've got something? I don't really want to go shopping."

"I know, you are the only woman I know who loathes shopping so much.

"Pretty much, I'd rather have bamboo shoved under my nails than try on a hundred stupid fitting dresses.

"Come over tonight, I'll get you set up with something."

Lizzy hung up and knew she wouldn't be able to concentrate on work! She checked the clock and made another call, "Hey Jennifer, it's me."

"Hello Chickadee, where the hell have you been? I haven't talked to you in almost a month," Jennifer said, happy to hear from her friend.

"I've got so much to tell you and I can't concentrate much on work. I've got to drop a packet over to a store later this morning, can you have lunch?"

"Happily I can. Where and when?"

"How about that soup and salad place we like, off Main."

"Sounds great, I'll see you there."

Lizzy couldn't wait to see Jennifer and catch her up on all the news. They usually saw each other weekly to hammer out some important psychological or spiritual issue but the last three weeks had been crazy. She was excited to get back on track. Jennifer always seemed to understand her.

Jennifer pulled up in her new red Honda. Jennifer had a giant white smile with cute little dimples and big brown eyes. Her real estate career had been taking off.

Lizzy waited inside, fidgeting, on the little sitting couch in the entryway. She gave Jennifer a big hug when she got inside.

"I don't know how three weeks went by so fast. You will not believe what has happened!" Lizzy said unable to contain her excitement.

The two women settled into their booth with their soup and salad. Lizzy launched into the story. Jennifer hung on every word. She couldn't believe her luck. She had been keeping something to herself for months and now that the subject of 'spirits' had been broached, she felt like she could tell Lizzy and not be ridiculed. She laughed heartily when Lizzy recounted meeting Officer Dan and her fashion faux pas.

"Oh Lizzy, only you!" she reached over and patted Lizzy's hand lightly.

"So, we sent Sunday into the light, left Josh at his office and dropped Tom back home," she sat back in the booth exhausted from talking so fast but exhilarated at the same time.

"Oh wait, one more thing! That 'Officer Dan' asked me to dinner," Lizzy blurted out.

Jennifer burst into laughter, "Oh Lizzy, that is hilarious! Are you going to go out with him?"

"Yes. Yes," Lizzy said, but made it clear she didn't want to get into it. She had more important issues to mull over with Jennifer, like moving souls from one dimension to the next. *Boys can wait*, she thought.

"Lizzy, you have to have some fun! You've always got yourself neck deep in some heavy subject whether it is your psychology or spirituality. I'm used to it, but you have got to learn to lighten up a little!" Jennifer looked straight into Lizzy's eyes and saw the wall. "Are you listening to me?"

"Yes, I hear you. Dan is taking me to the Royal Crown on Thursday night. I didn't want to go on Friday because, what if I don't like him? If I go on a Friday, there is no way to shake him off since the next day is Saturday. I've just always had such a hard time with first dates. It seems like they always last a little too long and get weird, whether I like the guy or not. The 'or not' is the worst, especially when you just want to go home and the date from hell thinks he wants to go home with you too."

"Oh shit! You're a crack up. I'm surprised you didn't tell him you'd meet him there," Jennifer said with a smirk. Lizzy's face dropped. "You did not tell him you would meet him there, did you?" Jennifer put her hands up to her face and began to laugh hysterically.

"Clearly I'm here on this earth for everyone's amusement!" Lizzy said completely embarrassed.

"Lizzy, it will be fine. Go to the Royal Crown and have some fun with 'Officer Dan'. I think its ok for him to know where you live. You'll be able to cut your date off by 10:00 o'clock if you want by saying you have to work. You've set it up nicely. You will be fine, but give the guy a chance already!"

Lizzy nodded and shrugged her shoulders, "I'll do my best."

"Listen, I know you're dying to get off this subject so let me talk to you about something that's been bothering me for quite some time. I felt weird telling you, or anyone for that matter because I thought maybe I was just letting my imagination get away with me. Now, after hearing your story, I feel a little better telling you my weird secret. I think I've got something going on at the house."

Lizzy sat straight up and leaned forward instantly intrigued, "Really? What is it?"

Jennifer lowered her voice. "This has been going on since I moved in last year with Gary. There is something in the corner of the bedroom. It's like a dark, shadowy mass. I can tell its there

126

because it blocks the lights from the window. That's the best way I can describe it. I wake up at night quite often to go the bathroom and when I get up and walk to the bathroom, it rushes to follow me to the door. At first, I thought it was my imagination even though I had the creepiest feeling, I just tried to ignore it. Lately, I've begun to feel intimidated by it. I'm getting so freaked out that I won't get up now. I just look at it from my bed when I wake up and decide if I want to deal with the challenge."

"I just can't believe you didn't tell me this a long time ago," said Lizzy.

"I know, but it's not something you just bring up in casual conversation."

"When have WE ever had casual conversation?" Lizzy said rolling her eyes.

"I didn't know how to bring it up. Even now, trying to describe the feeling and the situation is difficult. If I tell the wrong person they will think I'm crazy and sometimes that impression never goes away."

"Are you trying to tell me something?" Lizzy said as she grinned back at Jennifer.

"Oh shut up Lizzy! Everyone knows you're crazy and they're fine with it."

"What? Does everyone think I'm crazy?" This little tidbit actually alarmed Lizzy for a moment.

"No! I'm kidding, but, you are more complex than most and you are always into something," Jennifer didn't feel like calming Lizzy's insecurities at the moment.

"All right, all right," said Lizzy. "back to the subject. Can we go over to your house so I can get a feel for it?"

Lizzy had been to Jennifer's house many times before. Her home was tastefully furnished and decorated with brown and maroon colors. Lizzy had never picked up on anything strange in the house, although she had never been in Jennifer's room. Lizzy followed Jennifer home. She sat quietly on the corner of the bed with her eyes shut. Ten minutes drifted by and she wondered back into the living room and sat down with Jennifer.

"So, it's almost like," she paused, "well, I got the impression of a dog. A big dog like a German Shepherd, black, dark, I see how dark it is. I don't get a heavy negative feeling but I don't really get a positive one either. All I keep getting is 'the watcher',"

Jennifer's mouth hung open for a brief moment, "I felt that same thing! Why is it racing me to the bathroom door and intimidating me? This house is only a few years old so why is it here and where did it come from?"

"It's odd. I definitely get a strange feeling from it. I don't feel you are in danger, however, I also don't feel it is a positive energy for you to live with. I got an impression of a kind of soldier type guarding and watching this area. I don't know if your house is built on an area that he protected when alive or just what that impression is about. I've been diving in and studying spirit activity and a dark mass has never been a good spirit. There are some energys that are repeat, like a replay of a of an event. It is called residual energy and it does not recognize nor acknowledge the living. It is more like a recording. Then there are spirits trapped here who have decided for whatever reason not to move on into the light. Usually there is a mission or need to finish something or fix a situation. The feeling I'm getting in your room has a really strange vibe to it. I can't pinpoint it. I don't think I can get back over here before Friday to do a blessing. If you want it donet sooner, you could do it yourself."

"Huh uh, no, I'll wait for you," Jennifer was emphatic.

"Do you think you will be ok until then? I can do a blessing and see we'll see if we can move it out of here but I can't guarantee anything."

"Honestly, I will be fine. I haven't had a lot of sleep this last two weeks because of it. It seems to be escalating and getting more intense. I keep waking up around 3:00 a.m. and I can see it over there in the corner," Jennifer pointed back to her room. "I kind of don't open my eyes completely anymore. I check to see if it's there. It has been there every night this month. I just can't drink anything before I go to bed I guess! That will hopefully keep me from needing to go pee in the middle of the night. A couple more days is not going to kill me," Jennifer gave Lizzy her big white smile.

"I think it's strange that now that I've had this paranormal experience, I'm finding out about a lot of other people's experiences," Lizzy said as she stood up and walked to the corner of the room where the energy had been revealing itself.

"It is exciting too, isn't it?" asked Jennifer. "Maybe it's just law of attraction," Jennifer said as she motioned Lizzy back into the kitchen.

"I can't. I have to get back to work. I'm going to Karen's tonight to try on a couple of dresses for the big date Thursday." Her mind was tweaking, pushing, and trying to dial into what was happening in Jennifer's house. "Why would he take me to such a fancy restaurant on our first date?"

"Uh, maybe he's trying to impress you," Jennifer replied.

"Why though? The day he met me I had my shirt inside out, hardly any make up, basically I was a mess. It's not exactly a top ten list of women's traits that requires a dinner at the most expensive place in town. Plus, he's a cop. I thought they didn't make a lot of money to just be throwing around," Lizzy's cynical side raised it's ugly head. If she could figure a way to get out of this dinner she would but she knew her friends would kill her.

"Lizzy, police officers make a good living. I'm sure he doesn't go out like this all the time. He obviously means to make some kind of good impression on you. Stop analyzing it and just go and enjoy the dinner."

CHAPTER 18

Lizzy absolutely hated trying on clothes. She hated shopping more, so she prayed that Karen would have something she could wear. Dating was not at the top of her list just now. She had this new mission calling to her and she wasn't feeling the least bit romantic. On the other hand, it wasn't every day that a man tracked her down for a date.

Men baffled Lizzy. Any insecurities she had were exacerbated when she dated. She never felt pretty growing up or particularly special in any way. It didn't help that her mother was a stone cold beauty. Her tall, green eyed mother had always been thin with that 'California Girl' build. Lizzy was, in her opinion, short, medium build (or in her words 'stocky') and sort of average-looking in general. She tried to down play her curvaceous figure. In her 20's she decided that maybe she was not a wart on the ass of a pig. Lizzy remembered that this was a big step for her, this admission that she was not the wart on the ass of a pig.

Karen knew all the nuances of Lizzy and men after 25 years of friendship. Karen never understood why Lizzy was so insecure and hard on herself. She found it ridiculous that her friend was so blind to her own beauty while she always saw the beauty in her friends. Karen loved Lizzy and saw Lizzy in a much different light than Lizzy saw hereself. Lizzy's almond-shaped, hazel eyes and a bright smile could disarm almost anyone. Her sharp wit occasionally got her into hot water. She was downright hilarious when she relaxed. The problem was, she had a terrible time relaxing, especially on a date.

Karen never thought of her as "stocky". Lizzy's hour glass figure fit well on her 5'4" frame. Karen knew she had always wanted to be a tall, leggy blond. "Get over it, we can't all be models," Karen would tell her. "Bleach your hair and shut up already!"

The funny thing about Lizzy is she always was hard on herself regarding her shape and thought she looked bigger than she actually was. She and Karen wore the same size clothes and Lizzy just adored everything about Karen. She thought Karen always looked great and when Karen complained about her size, Lizzy would tell her she was crazy. Karen wondered how those two thought processes could exist in one person. How was it that Lizzy completely could not see herself?

Karen could see that men liked Lizzy but Lizzy was oblivious. When a man did flirt with her she either completely missed the cues or she fell apart like a 13 year old on their first date. Karen didn't understand it and love Lizzy in spite of her goofy behavior. Lizzy had seemed to gain some confidence over the last two years. Her last breakup made something snap and she sought counseling. Karen had noticed some good changes that came out of that experience.

Lizzy took pride in her appearance. She dressed conservatively with a flare of color and big jewelry. She had never gone in for manicures, pedicures and facials. It all seemed girlie and superfluous. It was all too much trouble to keep up, and it was darn expensive. She did enjoy a massage every few weeks, which was one indulgence she allowed herself on a regular schedule. She finally had found a hairstyle that was truly blow dry and go. Lizzy's impatience and constant drive was a thread through her life. Spirituality, loyalty and genuine love of her friends were other important threads woven into the design of her complex personality. Her compassionate heart seemed to get her hurt easily, although with age she was beginning to toughen up. In fact, now she seemed to lean a little more toward cynicism, especially where it came to love and relationships. She had not felt successful in her choices in men and found that when younger, she had fallen in love too easily and expected too little. She understood the choices she made had deeper psychological roots. *You marry your parents* she thought, *and it is a damn shame we recreate painful patterns throughout our lives until we mend the wounds.* She had not been married, but had a few long term, live-in relationships that ultimately didn't work out. Self-esteem issues had plagued her throughout her life and it tended to show up most when she was in relationship.

She had finally decided after the last break up that maybe she should give up on the whole idea of true love and romance. Hope springs eternal though, and Lizzy had worked very hard to heal the wounds that had diverted her in her life. Karen wasn't going to let her run away either. She was a hopeless romantic! Lizzy hoped she might choose better since she had spent some time after her last break up in therapy. She did feel stronger and more balanced. It all made her wonder if 'Officer Dan' was someone who would evolve into something more than a first date?

"Shake it off Lizzy, don't get sucked in! It's a date… A D-A-T-E, that's it," she said aloud as she stepped up to Karen's door.

Thank goodness, Karen's closet yielded a perfect little black dress. Lizzy arrived home around midnight and still felt keyed up. She took one more look at the dress, held it up in front of her, looked at it in the mirror and gave it another stamp of approval and then hung it carefully in the closet. Her 'dress' problem solved, her thoughts turned back to Jennifer. Her tight chest and stomach alerted her that she felt anxious about Jennifer's situation. She didn't want to wait to do the blessing, but had something going on every night of the week until Friday. She felt selfish and that made her feel bad. Should she have cancelled her date with Dan and helped her friend instead? Jennifer would have thought her ridiculous for even thinking it.

Lizzy tossed and turned unable to get comfortable or settle into sleep. She sighed, every time she looked at the clock, just to discover 15 minutes more had passed, 1:15 a.m., 1:30 a.m., 1:45 a.m. *This is absolutely maddening*, she thought. Finally, at 2:30

a.m. she turned on the light and sat up in bed. She prayed for Jennifer's safety and meditated on Jennifer and her family. She decided to do a remote house blessing.

Not knowing if it would work, she figured something would be better than nothing. She learned remote energy healing through her Reiki certification courses. In her studies to gain more insight spiritually, Lizzy had been ordained as a minister twice. The first time, she was enrolled in the Hypnotherapy Institute and at the conclusion of her certification was ordained through the school. The second time she was ordained through her mentor's church. She attended a rigorous year long, Ordination course of study which included gaining a certification as a Reiki Master.

Reiki, a powerful form of healing energy work, created a positive connection to the creator and flowed through the practitioner through to the subject. A Reiki Master is taught to perform energy work remotely. Lizzy had performed Reiki at a distance but never had tried anything like this. She made her mind quiet and began to pray. She imagined Jennifer's house in as much detail as possible as though she were there. She did her blessing and admonished any negative spirit or energy to leave the home. Lizzy imagined walking through Jennifer's house and performing the prayer and blessing in each room. She placed Reiki symbols of power, emotional healing and protection, in the corners of each room before she left for the next room. She blessed Jennifer's bedroom last. When she entered the room she brought down a stream of light from the heavens and surrounded her friend and her husband in a ball of light as they slept. She asked for protection and then blessed the room. Lizzy commanded that the "Watcher" to leave and did command it in the name of the Father, Son and Holy Spirit. She always brought a blessing in from the "Mother" as well because it never felt balanced in her mind if she didn't. She stayed mentally in the room as the next half hour passed. Finally, at the end, she brought in a very powerful clearing Reiki symbol and put it in the corner of the bedroom where the spirit had been living. She finished with an "Amen."

It was 4:00 a.m. and she didn't care. She felt so much better. There had been a gnawing feeling all day that the issue needed to be addressed immediately. She didn't know if the Reiki energy worked or if what she did had any effect but felt lighter now that she had prayed for her friend's protection. *Hopefully that will hold her until Friday when I can get there and do a formal blessing,* thought Lizzy as she snuggled into her pillow. She glanced at the clock one more time, 4:05 am. *Please let me fall asleep quickly.*

Tuesday, Lizzy's back to back appointments and evening training class pushed her arrival home past 8:00 p.m. Wednesday morning she found a moment and called Jennifer.

"Hey Jen, how's it going?"

"Really good, Chickade! How did the dress search go?" Jennifer was ready for plan B emergency shopping if Lizzy hadn't found a dress at Karen's.

"I found one, thankfully! It's a nice little black number, it should be just fine," Lizzy loved how considerate and caring Jennifer always seemed. *She's worried about my dress when she has some dark mass roaming around her bedroom! She is a true friend.*

"Enough about me, I wanted to call and see how things are in the bedroom," said Lizzy.

"Well, I never!" Jennifer laughed loudly. "What did you want to know about exactly? I am assuming you don't want naked details."

"Oh my God! I don't want any naked details whatsoever you kook! I'm talking about the dark thing in your bedroom not your husband!" Jennifer always knew how to get her going.

"Actually," Jennifer said in a low serious tone, "It's gone."

"What do you mean it's gone? How can you be sure?"

"I've been living with this thing for months. It's gone I tell you. The room feels better, no being chased to the loo, no dark shadow thing in the corner, it's gone. I woke up to go pee Monday night and checked around and it was gone. Last night, same thing, woke up as usual around 3:30 am and it was not there. I could see all the lights coming in the window and I was not met at the bathroom door by Dark Fido!"

"That is actually pretty exciting because I stayed up Monday night. I couldn't sleep; I was so worried about you. I prayed and did a 'spiritual walk through' of your home. After we talked, I just had an uneasy feeling I could not shake. I couldn't get over there until Friday, so I decided to pray for your protection and I did an a remote walk through blessing of your home. I used Reiki energy and around 4:00 a.m. called it a done deal. I was hoping it would help somehow since Friday seemed decades away!"

"Whatever you did, worked! I feel so much better and even though I still woke up at 3:30 am, I was able to go right back to sleep. I slept soundly for the first time in months. Last night I had the same pleasant experience. Thank you so much Lizzy!"

"Maybe I can come with you on some of your cases," Jennifer said. She wanted in on the action.

"Cases? I don't have cases! I did help with the Sunday Stewart incident simply because it affected Karen first. I wanted to help you because you are dear to me and I can't have shadowy figures roaming around your room, if I can help stop it. I certainly don't have cases!" Lizzy tantalized by the idea knew she did want "cases".

"You want to be a ghost hunter, Jennifer?" Lizzy said with a little sarcasm in her tone.

"I want to help and I'm fascinated by it all," Jennifer replied, ignoring the tone.

"Ok, but you weren't even willing to do your own house blessing without me being there. So, you are telling me that you are willing to go into strangers' houses to seek out paranormal issues?"

"So? It's different when it's your own...haunting," Jennifer said. She felt justified in the apprehension she felt doing her own blessing.

"I've been tormented for months by that thing. I didn't feel strong enough, I guess, to handle it myself. I'm not sure I even knew I could do something until we talked. I think it is a perfect example of why you need to continue this work."

"What do you mean?" Lizzy asked.

"Well, I'm a normal every day person who found myself in a strange situation that I didn't know how to handle it. The we talked and I felt some hope. I'm sure there are others out there who are going through the same emotions and confusion."

"I agree that it is different when it is happening to you. Karen was with Janet and I when we kind of got sucked into 'Sunday's case' if you will. We finished with it and Karen announced that she is not interested in pursuing any type of ghost or paranormal investigating."

"Why?" Jennifer was baffled that Karen didn't want to be part of something so spectacular.

"She feels like there is too much drama and risk. After the experience with Sunday's spirit attaching to so many different people, she doesn't want to take the chance of accidently bringing something home."

"Hmmm, I do see her point but I think the opportunity to help people and souls, outweighs that for me. Aren't there ways for us to protect ourselves from things attaching to us?"

"I don't know all the in's and out's, Jennifer. I would think as long as we bless ourselves and ask for strength and protection, we should be able to ward off hitchhikers. That said, I'm no expert on this. I've only started researching the subject deeply this last month or so when all this happened. I don't want to endanger anyone or cause something to happen where a spirit attaches to them and then torments them or their family. That's a lot of responsibility."

"In other words, proceed at your own risk," said Jennifer.

"Yes," said Lizzy, her excitement growing with the thought of having Jennifer on board.

Jennifer had been raised Catholic and like many Catholics had pulled away from the Church after feeling judged. Her spiritual core and devotion was strong.

"All right, when or if I have something come up, I will call you and Janet and we'll see what we can see, and do what we can do," said Lizzy.

"Wow, you're profound," Jennifer said with a snicker. "I've gotta go. Good luck with Officer Dan tomorrow."

"Don't remind me!"

The idea of squeezing into the little black dress and making small talk all night with a cop sounded like as much fun as slamming her hand in a door at the moment.

What should I do if he asks about Karen's incident? What in the world am I supposed to tell him? I was at my friend's side to help her through a ghostly encounter. Sounds ridiculous, no wonder no one talks about their experiences, they think everyone will think they are crazy. Lizzy forced herself to think of something else before she went crazy.

CHAPTER 19

A couple of minutes before 7:00 p.m. Lizzy thought maybe she would luck out and Dan wouldn't show. It wasn't like she hadn't been stood up before. In her early 20's it became a game it got so bad. She always had secondary plans. Just when she was thinking she might be in the clear, Dan pulled up in a black Chevy Camaro.

Really? she thought, *I love that car!*

Dan stood about 5' 11" with light brown hair and big brown eyes. Yes, Lizzy had noticed the day she met him at Karen's house. She was sure he whitened his teeth because when he smiled he glowed; not in a bad way, but a little bit in a 'let me kiss your baby' political kind of way. He was built like a brick. She had to admit, she liked it. Suddenly, her stomach leapt up and did a summersault.

"Shit," she whispered to herself as she watched the hunk of Dan walk up to her door, "now I'm nervous."

She opened the door, Dan stood on the other side with a big white shining grin, holding out a single yellow rose.

"My Lady," Dan said with a silly English accent.

"Oh, thank you. It's beautiful."

"You look beautiful! Yellow is for a new beginning and happiness, I thought it was appropriate," Dan motioned her to the car.

Lizzy fumbled around as she locked her front door. She felt completely self-conscious, stomach in a knot, Lizzy turned and walked to the car pretending to be confident.

"You look very gallant yourself by the way," she said as she grabbed his arm.

The dark charcoal suit with a red silk tie set off Dan's tan skin and blond hair. Dan opened Lizzy's door and she slid inside.

"Your car makes me giddy," Lizzy blurted out.

"How so?"

"This is my favorite car, although I would want a white one. I go online sometimes and fantasize about it," Lizzy caught herself talking really fast. *Whoa Nellie, slow it down he's just a guy*, she said to herself as she patted the side of her leg.

"I love it too, that's why I bought it! Lizzy, you look very nice. Thank you for accepting my invitation. I didn't think you would call to be completely honest," he looked over at Lizzy with his big brown eyes. "I asked you to call me the first day we met but you didn't."

"Well, you said to call if we heard anything or figured out who was in Karen's house and we didn't hear anything. I mean, we kind of did, but it wasn't phone call worthy."

"Wait a minute, you know who was in the house?" Dan's head whipped around and Lizzy could see he was concerned.

"Uhm, wait a minute, let's not talk about that just yet," Lizzy said. "I mean, I didn't realize you were interested in me and that's why I didn't call."

"Huh, I gave out all the signals. Your friend Karen got it."

"I'm not Karen," Lizzy said in a very staccato rhythm.

"I didn't mean anything by it. I just meant, I was giving out the signals and I had hoped you would call."

"Dan, where it comes to men and dating I'll just lay my cards on the table, I'm thick. So it's best to be very clear with me about what you want, because if you are being coy there is a good chance I'll miss it."

"Hmmm, as intense and detailed as you were at your friend's house I'm a little surprised that you missed the clues."

"I was a little surprised by all of this. I looked a wreck that day and of course, my charm became obvious, I'm sure, when you noticed my shirt was inside out! Lord help me!"

"You were very sweet. It was clear you had rushed over there. I watched you take care of your friend and I could just tell you had a good heart and I just liked what I saw," Dan said.

"It's weird," Lizzy said rolling her eyes.

"Well dear, you clean up pretty nice anyway," Dan laughed and patted her on the knee and then left his hand there for the rest of the trip to the restaurant.

Lizzy's heart pounded under her little black dress. She could hear its rhythm in her own ears.

"Now tell me what you heard about your friend's intruder," Dan nudged back to the subject Lizzy was trying so hard to avoid.

"Dan, this is a first date and if I go into it you're going to think I'm off balance," Lizzy sighed and felt she could see the date ending before it even started.

"Nonsense! Tell me what you know little lady."

"How about I tell you over dinner since we are almost there."

The host, dressed in a tuxedo, seated the couple at a lovely table by a window overlooking the mountains. The Royal Crown sat on top of one of the taller hillsides in the county. It overlooked the valley and the mountains. The setting sun cast brilliant colors across the valley. The restaurant planted a Royal Garden on the grounds around the building. Lizzy thought it looked like something out of the renaissance. As the weather got warmer, local musicians played on the large stone patio. "This place is lovely," Lizzy said admiring the whole package.

Lizzy could see Dan, the cop, waiting for the rundown on Karen and Lizzy's discovery of who had been in the house.

"All right Dan, buckle up it's going to be a bumpy ride," she said with a slight grin on her face. She slowly began the story of Sunday Stewart, the hitchhiking ghost.

Dan listened intently. Lizzy couldn't tell if he believed her or wanted to cancel dinner and take her straight home.

"It's a very interesting story, Lizzy and it is clear you believe that it happened."

"So you don't believe me?" Lizzy tried not to be disappointed.

"It's not that I don't believe you, I just don't believe in that kind of stuff. I believe there is a logical explanation for all of it and it doesn't include ghosts."

"Really? You think there is a logical explanation" Lizzy said obviously annoyed. "You believe that some kids broke into Karen's house, turned all the water on, took all the pictures off the walls and put her chairs in the living room in the symbol of a cross? This is logical to you?" Lizzy did not hide her exasperation.

"Lizzy, the answer is yes. That could have happened. They may have been trying to make it look 'ghostly'."

"So, you think the same kids beat us over to Tina's house? Then, they motored on over to Tom and Deanna Hoskins before we got there too? Dan, I know what I experienced when we were at Josh's office. I also know that no one is having any more paranormal trouble since we helped move Sunday into the light. That's what I know."

"Lizzy, I don't think you're crazy, ok. I just don't believe in ghosts. I am sure many of the things that have happened have a perfectly logical explanation. Is this difference of opinion going to ruin my chances for a second date?"

Lizzy wasn't sure, but she could have sworn that Dan actually batted his thick lashed brown eyes at her. She had to admit, it did kind of melt her inside. This was not anything she wanted to get in the way of a potential relationship.

"You want a second date?" asked Lizzy.

"I'd like it to be an option," Dan replied.

"I would like to see you again" said Lizzy. "That said, I want to be completely upfront, I plan to pursue this Ghost Investigation and House Cleansing endeavor. If it is going to bother you we should probably go our separate ways, don't you think?" asked Lizzy.

"You can ghost hunt all you want Lizzy, it is neither here nor there to me," Dan said with a shrug. "I don't see any reason for it to impede us getting to know each other better."

Lizzy felt relieved when hearing it. As much as she wanted to avoid the whole date, she now found herself, of course, liking him after all.

Lizzy thought she heard someone calling her name. She looked up as Josh Stewart approached the table with a tall, beautiful blond woman. His dark blue suit set off his black hair and blue eyes. *'Eye candy',* flitted through Lizzy's thoughts. They both looked sharp. Of course, everyone at the Royal Crown looked great, as they were dressed to the nines.

"Lizzy, I thought that was you. I can't believe I've run into you here!" Josh said as he strode up to the table smiling ear to ear. "I'm sorry to interrupt. I'm Josh Stewart and this is my wife Cynthia." He reached out and shook Dan's hand.

"Hello," said Cynthia politely and then took a step back. Her jaw set and not looking pleased.

That's his wife? Oh my God, she's beautiful! Lizzy thought and felt immediately like an ugly stepsister.

"I'm Dan."

"You've got quite a girl here Dan, but I'm sure you know that already."

"You're a little far from home aren't you?" Lizzy said, breaking in quickly to what could become an awkward conversation. "You live over an hour away. I'm surprised to see you here."

"I know and what a lucky coincidence!" Josh said loudly.

It appeared to Lizzy that Josh was a little buzzed.

Josh kept smiling and looked directly into Lizzy's eyes. "Cynthia and I looove this place so we try to make the trek at least once a month." He slid his card over to Lizzy, "Did you get my message today?"

"Message? No, when did you leave it," asked Lizzy.

"Oh, just before we left for dinner."

Lizzy took the card and put it into her purse. She caught the look of irritation on Dan's face.

"It is so weird you're here..." Josh trailed off for a moment. "Anyway, please call me tomorrow, if it's convenient. I have a client I need to discuss with you and I feel it is an urgent matter."

"Sure, I'll call you in the morning." There it was, an awkward pause Lizzy had been attempting to circumvent. Josh reached his hand back searching for Cynthia. "All right, you two have a lovely dinner."

"Who was that?" Dan asked once they were out of range.

"That is Sunday's brother, Josh, who I was just telling you about."

"The therapist?" Dan asked, his face softening.

"Yes, the therapist. That's enough of all this Dan, how about you tell me a little about yourself. I've dominated the conversation with tales of ghosts, life after death and paranormal activity. Let's bring it back down to earth. So, you're a cop..."

Dan smiled and launched into an hour report about his journey as a police officer and his plans to move up the ranks and hopefully make Chief someday.

The rest of the evening clicked by smoothly. Lizzy relaxed and ended up having fun in spite of herself. Dan politely walked her to her door and there they were. This is the most awkward part of a date and Lizzy hated it. Lizzy felt like she was 14 again. All she wanted to do was run into the house. Dan reached over guided

Lizzy's chin up and gave her a soft kiss. "Thank you for a very nice evening."

"It was nice, Dan, thank you as well."

"May I have your number?" Dan finally asked.

"My number? Oh, of course!" Lizzy had forgotten that all the communication had been passed through Karen and she had called him. Lizzy scribbled her personal cell number on her business card and handed it to Dan.

"All right my dear, I'll be calling. Now in you go, safe and sound," the silly British accent was back with a smile.

"Good night Dan," Lizzy curtsied and slowly shut the door. *Was it too late to call Karen? Yes, but it's not too late to send her a quick text.* Lizzy fumbled around on her phone and sent Karen a quick message. "I had a wonderful time, thanks for lending me the dress. Call me in the morning."

Lizzy crawled into bed and ran the night's events through her mind. *Would he call?* She doubted it. *Did I do anything stupid?* She didn't think she had. *What client could Josh want to speak about? Wouldn't that a breach of confidentiality? What is the meaning of Life?* She cracked herself up and began laughing.

"Yeah, what *is* the meaning of life?" she said into her empty room.

Lizzy could feel change coming. She knew she would not stop the Ghost Investigation endeavor. She didn't feel she was 'chasing ghosts'. Lizzy felt she was ushering spirits to a better place and helping the families who were living with them. Other than that, she didn't know what the future held. Who does? She decided she would call Josh first thing in the morning. She said a prayer of thanks and protection for herself, friends and family. She drifted off to sleep thinking about Dan's ultra-bright smile and big brown eyes.

CHAPTER 20

A quaint brick, ranch style home, sat on an acre at 7504 Devonshire Lane. Surrounded by trees, its well-manicured lawn looked like an emerald laying in front of the house. The newly-married Andersons had moved in the month before.

Stacy, her new husband Jack and her son sat balled up in the corner of the living room. She didn't know what it was but "Banshee" came to mind. It was all white with a large skeletal head and it flying, racing in circles through the living room. It was not happy, not happy at all. The thing was enraged. It appeared to have long flowing hair but the face was anything but beautiful. Empty eye sockets and teeth bared, it stopped in front of them. It unhinged its jaw and let out a scream. The family covered their ears and closed their eyes. Stacy could swear she felt her hair actually blow back. Jack had no idea what was happening. He did his best to move in front of his family in an attempt to protect them. Just as quickly as it started, it ended. The room went quiet. It was so quiet. The three huddled and hugged each other.

"What the hell was that?" Jack yelled. "We all saw it right?"

Stacy and her son Brian couldn't speak but nodded their heads tears running down their faces.

"Come on, get in the car we're leaving," Jack grabbed the keys and pushed his family out through the front door. They loaded up into their trusty van and sped to Stacy's mother's house a few miles away.

About The Author

Daria Kacie grew up in the Northwest. Many of the incidents and stories portrayed in her books are based on true events. She has studied Metaphysics and the Paranormal her whole life. Daria has a deep sense of spirit and constantly looks for the magic in her world. She is excited to share her experiences and knowledge with her readers. She continues to live in the Northwest with her husband.

One Last thing

Thanks for reading! If you enjoyed this book, I'd be grateful if you'd post a short review on Amazon. Your support does make a difference. I personally read all reviews so I can get your feedback to make my books better.

If you would like to write a review please visit me at Author Central.

Join Our Reader List

If you would like to receive special offers and updates on new titles being released please sign up here:

Quantumlifepublishing.com.

Thank you for your support!

~Daria Kacie